The Five Year Old Man

Debashish

Become Shakespeare.com

First published in 2018 by

Becomeshakespeare.com

Wordit Content Design & Editing Services Pvt Ltd
Unit - 26, Building A -1, Nr Wadala RTO,
Wadala (East), Mumbai 400037, India
T: +91 8080226699

Wordit Art Fund helps deserving authors publish
their work by providing monetary support.
To apply for funding, please visit us at
www.BecomeShakespeare.com

©

ISBN - 978-93-88081-39-9

Dedication

This book is dedicated to
"La Seine"

Acknowledgement

I would like to take this opportunity to acknowledge the influence and inspiration I received from the classical and modern science fiction literature, Television series and movies.

The narrative of this book is inspired by the works of Mary Shelley, Isaac Asimov and Anime like 'Ghost in the shell' and 'Alita battle angel'. Also, this book draws inspiration from movies like 'Enthiran'. Watching countless hours of documentaries on Nat Geo and The Discovery Channel has helped me to create a plausible version of the future. At last, I would humbly conclude that If I have been able to see ahead, It is only by standing on the shoulders of Giants.

Contents

Chapter 1	7
Chapter 2	15
Chapter 3	20
Chapter 4	25
Chapter 5	31
Chapter 6	37
Chapter 7	43
Chapter 8	49
Chapter 9	58
Chapter 10	65
Chapter 11	71
Chapter 12	77
Chapter 13	83
Chapter 14	89
Chapter 15	96
Chapter 16	106
Chapter 17	111
Chapter 18	116
Chapter 19	123
Chapter 20	130

Chapter 21   136

Chapter 22   143

Chapter 23   147

Chapter 24   154

Chapter 25   161

Chapter 26   168

Chapter 27   174

Chapter 28   180

Chapter 29   186

Chapter 30   193

Chapter 31   199

Chapter 32   206

Chapter 33   214

Chapter 34   223

Chapter 35   231

Ten years later   236

The facts behind the fiction   241

Chapter 1

Dr Vankateshwara straightened his tie as he analysed his overall appearance in the mirror for the last time before the interview. A form-fitted crisp suit with an ironed shirt, blue tie, tailor-made pants and formal shoes, clean-shaven face accompanied by salt and pepper hair gave an impression of intellectual superiority. For he was intelligent enough to earn two doctorates at a comparatively young age but smart enough to know that none of that mattered unless he looked the part before the camera. Then he reached for his spectacle from the bedside table, put it on and pushed it higher by its nose bridge.

"Come on; you have faced worse." He said to his reflection staring back at him as he exhaled deeply. Then, he confidently walked towards his study where the reporter was waiting. His past experiences have made him better prepared for today, at least that's what he thought. Nevertheless, he was confident that this was his day and he was ready to amaze the world with his achievement. As he grabbed the doorknob to his study, he took a deep breath to calm his nerves and put on a vibrant smile before pushing the door open.

"Hello Dr Venkatesh, it's a pleasure to meet you again," Susan Phillip greeted with a smile.

"Oh, the pleasure is all mine Susan, sorry to keep you waiting," Venkatesh replied with an enthusiastic grin, perhaps a little too enthusiastic. He had chosen the study as the location of the interview because of its décor. The extensive collection of books it held on topics like robotics, A.I and psychology and an antique oak table topped with red velvet gave the impression of a well-read gentleman.

Susan however, got an immediate impression of a nervous wreck who was trying to overcompensate. Someone who didn't want to be argued with and wanted his words to carry weight. She had chewed and spat such elites in the past without giving a second thought; she wasn't going to make an exception today.

Venkatesh sat in his chair across the table, just opposite to Ms Phillips, a prime position that instigates arguments. The cameraman and the sound guy got busy with their final preparations, clipped on a collar mike on Dr Venkateshwara's suit. The wise doctor sat there patiently, his arms resting on the armrest of his chair, gauging the predator-like instinct in the reporter's eye. "Not today," he thought to himself as a smug smile formed on his lips.

"So, we record in 5, 4, 3, 2, 1" Susan ended the countdown with her first question.

"Dr Venkatesh, you understand that we serve to the average, everyday folks and not academicians. So why did you choose us for this exclusive interview?"

"You see Ms Susan, our research has the potential to affect the lives of everyone on this planet and their future, so it is only justified that I explain it to ordinary everyday people as best as I can because after all; knowledge is meant to be shared," Venkatesh replied with a smile.

"Before we go into a more technical aspect of it, will you kindly illustrate why do we need a conscious A.I? I mean when we already have advanced A.I capable of replacing factory workers in the industries, what is the necessity of a self-conscious robot apart from a novelty?" Susan asked with a pretence of innocence.

"You see, even though we have the necessary A.I capability to free people from their mundane, repetitive jobs so that they can invest their time elsewhere." Vankatesh began tactfully. " We are still not able to exploit the full capability of A.I since a robot can be only as useful as it is intelligent. Being self-conscious will not only help a robot do its job well but also guide him to choose an objective without human interference, and above all; by replicating consciousness in a machine, we will understand our consciousness better."

"So according to my research, there have been many projects in the past by various scientists who have attempted to replicate the consciousness of the human mind inside a computer, many have succeeded in different aspects, how is your work different from them?" Susan inquired.

"Subtly, you see we have built upon their work; the problem was the previous attempts were made to have a self-conscious A.I without a self. Humans wrote all the millions of lines of codes governing the mind of the machines; we attempt to change that." Venkatesh explained.

"Dr Vankateshwar, are you saying that your experimental A.I will be able to program and reprogramme itself ?" Her eyes were shining with a strange light of impatience as if she was waiting for Venkatesh to step into the trap. He sensed it, but lying wasn't an option. A self-adapting and reprogramming A.I was too big an achievement in his career to hide for fear of a pesky reporter.

"You see Ms Susan, for an A.I to be conscious, it has to adapt to new situations which are far from ideal, not only will it need to learn new skills but also acquire new ways of interacting with different circumstances and people. As these situations can be drastically different, hence one's set of rules may not successfully apply to the other and hence, fluidity is a must. We humans, do it all the time. Depending on where we are, with whom, we reprogram our behaviour and even our thoughts because we are conscious of our surroundings and always reacting and adapting to it. These are essential for any conscious being." Venkatesh emphasised with occasional nods.

"Do you intend this A.I of yours to interact with people like your previous experiment, 'Project Turing'?" A malicious smile was sitting on her lips; she had hit him where it hurts. The pangs of pain that Venkatesh felt were barely hidden from the camera as Venkatesh suddenly flinched in his chair, for Project Turing was his failure, but so what? Who doesn't fall, who doesn't fail? Success comes to those who dare to get up and run again, and that's what Venkatesh was going to do. He exhaled deeply to calm himself before answering.

"Project Turing is in the past, and it would be better if we let it be, as for your question, No! We are not going to repeat the same mistake twice. This time the human interaction will be limited and carefully monitored. The A.I will initially interact with only me and the team of mine and slowly will its social circle grow as we see fit."

"Ah! So you will parent the A.I, overcompensating for something Dr Vankateshwara?" She remarked with a sly smile. "Anyway my question is, what if this A.I outsmarts you to escape its limited social freedom? I am sure your brainchild will be a smart one and what if it escapes your guidance before it is ready, what mayhem can an angry teenage young robot not cause; I wonder?"

"Another reference to angry teenagers, is she deliberately trying to bring up the Turing incident or am I just imagining stuff?" Venkatesh contemplated while he took a quick glance at the cameraman and then looked back at Susan. " Ms Susan, you make it sound like I am trying to adopt our new project." he burst into mock laughter. "I personally never thought of it this way, but you see, this one is programmed like an infant. Even though it has the resources to perform vast calculations, but it is limited because it has not been programmed to do more than what an infant does; in fact, less. With time it will learn new things including locomotion and language, and at this initial stage it will program itself the way we want it to because it has been programmed to trust people based on their interaction with it, so yes; it is pretty much like nurturing a child…" Susan interrupted before Venkatesh could finish.

"And you believe you will be able to be a good parent to the most 'potentially dangerous' child on the planet, and that too without any prior experience."

"Nobody understands this most 'potentially useful' child better than us." Venkatesh defended.

" Is it programmed with the three laws of robotics ?" Susan asked.

"Oh! You mean Asimov's three laws? Not entirely, it is programmed to follow only the first and the last law, nobody can have free will until they are free to disobey orders, can they?" Venkatesh asked rhetorically.

"So you plan to create a robot that can learn like a human, is exponentially faster at learning than almost every human, can reprogram itself as it sees fit and does not need to obey anyone. Dr Vamkateshwara, do you not think that this is a pretty dangerous combination and the only thing we hope will prevent it from going rogue and turning into 'Skynet' are your parenting skills? A man who has never fathered a child before?" Susan Jibed and her comment had served its desired purpose, Venkatesh was silent. The way she had put it made his work seemed like a recipe for disaster. How could he possibly provide an answer that could satisfy her and her paranoid dim-witted patrons, he had to think of something smart because he knew that public opinion could sabotage the greatest of scientific advancement. No wonder he was cursing the moment he agreed to this stupid idea of an exclusive interview with Susan Philip, the most sensational and hence popular news anchor he had known. He was a scientist, not a P.R agent and no amount of practice interview and rehearsals in front of the mirror could have prepared him for this moment. But his intellectual pride was too much for him to admit it. He leaned back in his chair, turned it at a slight angle away from her as he interlocked his fingers.

"I see your points are fear-driven, and even though there is a small possibility that it can come true but trust me, we can pull the 'plug' off anytime we want. In fact, the project will be self-terminated if one of my teammates doesn't regularly check in on it." Venkatesh continued with genuine humility "Yes! It is true that the A.I is capable of immeasurable destruction like a human being, but as long as a scholarly team of PhDs are there to guide its limitless potential, you can sleep easy that bigotry, hatred or hypocrisy won't corrupt it. I admit that certain dangers are there and that would be enough to make us cautious of the future development of our project." Venkatesh assured with a slight bow of his head.

"So you admit that your project is dangerous and..." Venkatesh interfered before she could complete "Ms Susan, do you have to be repetitive and redundant, please move on to your next question. I am a busy man."

Susan stared blankly at the doctor with an ajar mouth for a while. Then, after regaining her composure, she spoke. "No, Dr Venkateshwara, I think that would be all, thank you for your time. The interview will be on tonight's prime time." Susan announced in a formal tone and signed her team for a pack-up. When the collar mike was taken off Venkatesh, Susan leaned forward against the table.

"Dr Venkatesh! I am not against scientific progress, but you must learn that you have a greater responsibility than the blind pursuit of knowledge and be aware of its consequences on the lives of others."

Chapter 2

Venkatesh was sitting in a restaurant a few blocks away from his lab. He planned to buy lunch for his core team who were busy running final diagnostic check-ups before activating the A.I. While he was waiting for the order to arrive his mind was pondering about what Susan said to him. As a scientist, he always thought that it was not just his job but his responsibility to pursue knowledge. To venture into the unknown so that the Human knowledge could be advanced. He always treated films about robot apocalypse as a product of the fear of the human mind of the unknown, what if the fear wasn't baseless? Like many another philosopher, he considered non-aggression as a trait of a more enlightened mind, what if aggression was the key to survival, wouldn't then a superior intelligence choose to be aggressive for a better chance of survival? He would have kept pondering such questions, but the vibrating cell phone in his pocket derailed his chain of thoughts. The name displayed was of Dr Anna Ainsworth.

Dr Ainsworth was a developmental Psychologist and specialised in child psychoanalysis. She met Venkatesh a few years back, at a seminar about the psychology of consciousness and the recent development in the field. Venkatesh, realising her expertise about the working and development of a child's mind and admiring her tall, slender figure and curly red hair couldn't help but to ask her out on a date and ask her in on his research. She agreed to one of his propositions, and they have been working together ever since. Venkatesh considered himself fortunate to have found a good friend and a brilliant colleague like her, not that he wasn't looking for more, but he was satisfied with what he had.

He picked up the phone to be asked by Shen in his best bugs bunny impression "Whats up Doc? You bringing me a carrot cake?" Shen Jiamo, like the other two of the team, was a doctorate of none and the only philosophy that he could relate to was the polar opposite of what Venkatesh's father used to tell him while growing up "high living, Simple thinking." Now of course, for Shen, a high life meant a life high in calories. Venkatesh always found himself to be a little envious of Shen, no matter how much or what he ate, it seemed he was incapable of gaining weight. Now before anyone assumes Shen to be a stereotypical Asian comic relief of the team (which they won't be entirely wrong to assume.), it will be beneficial to note that he was a brilliant engineer with masters in Mechatronics. Shen was the one who created the robotic shell for Dr Venkatesh's A.I so that it could process the world as a human would. Even though he was less qualified than the other two, he considered his contribution to the secret Chinese space project enough to compensate for that, which of course he had no proof of considering the secret nature of the project.

"Today is not your birthday Shen, as far as I remember," Venkatesh remarked with deadpan humour. "Why are you calling from Anna's phone?"

"He discharged his own while building himself a virtual empire." Came the voice of Anna, the phone was of course on speaker. "When will you be coming? we need to run a final check on the learning and adapting algorithm."

"Pretty soon. I will be on my way as soon as I pick up the order" Said Venkatesh while checking his watch.

"What are you bringing Doc?" Shen asked curiously.

"Something edible and in generous quantity for the three of us, I assume that would be adequate info for you." Venkatesh teased.

"Aye Aye captain! By the way, what do you want to set the response for Fat, alcohol, salt and sugar in the spectral analyser, and what magnitude?" Shen asked.

"Set it positive 60% for sugar, 30 for salt, maybe 5 to 10 for fat, make it 5, and set Alcohol to negative 30%." Instructed Venkatesh as Shen jotted down the parameters.

"No, set it to positive 50 for fat. Venkatesh just because you are on a diet doesn't mean it can't enjoy occasional ice-creams and Chips, humans love the taste of fat and have been eating it since prehistory. It's sugar that you should keep a watch out for." Anna warned him.

"Very well, pamper the A.I all you want, 50% it is," Venkatesh affirmed.

"You don't want the A.I to enjoy some vintage Kentucky bourbon on a rainy night by the fireplace Doc?" Shen asked with a melodramatic sorrowful voice.

"Mr Shen, have you been drinking since you were 5?" Venkatesh asked with annoyance.

"I wish my old man had allowed, what a splendid childhood it would have been." Shen retorted. " But as you say, boss! Come quick and bring the food quicker, bye!"

"Oh wait! How was the interview with Susan Phillip, When are they gonna broadcast it?" Anna asked enthusiastically.

"I don't think they will; they can't show manslaughter on news network, can they?" Shen commented with a pretence of disappointment before Venkatesh could reply.

"It was nothing of that sort Shen. We were both mature adults, behaving professionally and discussing the experiment." Venkatesh explained in a calm, diplomatic voice.

" Ya, she screwed you like a pro, didn't she?" Anna jibed, and Shen burst into a fit of laughter.

" I knew an exclusive with Susan Phillip was a terrible idea." Venkatesh let out a sigh " Curse the moment when I agreed to it and on the person who suggested it."

"Told you not to go drinking with the chairman!" Anna exclaimed triumphantly. "See you later professor."

" Ok Bye! The order is ready, got to go." Venkatesh replied in a hurry.

"See your Doc," said Shen quickly before Venkatesh disconnected. Then he went to the receptionist where the order was waiting at the table, paid for it. Put the phone in his pocket, left out of the door and then suddenly recalled that he forgot to pick up the order. He hurriedly went back to pick it up beamed a silly smile at the receptionist and headed towards his bicycle.

Chapter 3

Venkatesh and Shen were busy with the final preparations before activating the A.I. Shen was running simulations for the tactile response of the Androids artificial skin whereas Venkatesh was debugging the last few hundreds of lines of the code when Anna walked into the lab with a large box of piping hot pizza.

The lab was a spacious one cluttered with all sort of machines, from 3D printers to CNC Lathe and Miller while on the opposite end laid the computers where Shen had designed the robotic shell, Venkatesh was sitting on the other end of the Lab on his System. Near about the Centre of the Lab was a plastic Chair on which the lifeless Android sat with a placid expression. It's Fibre composite skeleton and actuators were covered by a grey coloured artificial skin with an embedded grid of shiny silvery piezo-electric wires. Only its face and hands were covered with synthetic human-like silicone skin as Venkatesh considered functionality and economic feasibility more important than vanity. Its head was bald and so was its face, lacking any facial hair excluding the fake eyelashes. Its face was modelled after a 3D composite image of the faces of its three creators, one of whom had left his station and rushed towards the pizza as soon as it's delicious cheesy aroma reached him.

"You should have seen his interview," Anna suggested to Shen while looking at Venkatesh. "It wasn't as bad as the doctor made it out to be, I would say he managed it well… Watch out, Shen! Thin crust!" Even before Shen could realise, a significant portion of cheese and toppings had slipped off the pointy edge of the slice, which he was holding at the crust and fell on the floor.

"wastage of perfectly good pizza! that's an omen from the gods." Shen warned sarcastically, "And I have decided it. I am not putting 'worked with Dr Venkatesh Iyer' on my resume. Period." Shen commented as he chewed on the remaining toppings and cheese on his decimated slice.

"If you guys are done, could you please put on the eyebrows and hair on it Anna! Finish with your simulations if you don't want to sleep in this lab Shen!" Instructed Venkatesh from the far end of the lab.

"Who doesn't cheer up in the presence of pizza?" Shen asked with his mouth full.

" You know who." Anna rolled her eyes toward Vankatesh as both went to finish off their respective tasks.

About an hour later, all three of them were standing close together in front of the Android and looking at it.

"Do you guys think it will be the right time, or should we wait until the morning?" Venkatesh looked at them nervously.

"Doc, the simulations are perfect, and unless you doubt your coding skills, I guess it is ready to rise and shine; or kill, depending on your codes." Shen shrugged.

"Are we going to refer to the A.I as "it"? I think it deserves a name." Anna declared.

"What do you mean?" Venkatesh's eyes narrowed in surprise. "it already has a name, the name of our project, Artificial Intelligent Simulation of Human Awareness and Consciousness, A.I.S.H.A.C for short."

"Seriously Doc?" Shen asked in surprise. "How big of a nerd do you have to be to name an android as an acronym?"

"What? It makes perfect sense. A.I.S.H.A.C is our project, this is our project, and hence this is A.I.S.H.A.C." Venkatesh explained while pointing at the android.

"Isaac! That's what it should be. 'Isaac'!" Anna suggested, snapping her fingers.

"Cool! Isaac as in Isaac Newton and Isaac Asimov. Nerdy enough for the Doc, sciency enough for the droid." Shen affirmed while fist bumping Anna.

"Yes! Isaac is a good name..." Venkatesh was interrupted before he could finish.

"And therefore, it shall be the name of the A.I." Anna declared! " uh, uh uh, no if, no buts" she shut Venkatesh before he could object.

"Fine! But are you guys sure we should wake him up now? I mean…" Vankatesh was interrupted again by Anna before he could finish.

"Look at him! The doctor is as nervous as a first-time father!" Anna mocked while pinching both of Venkatesh's cheeks. "That's so cute!"

"It's nothing like that." Venkatesh said, trying to brush off his awkwardness. " I think we should double check the codes one last time."

"Doc, you have already triple checked and debugged the codes, go ahead man! We trust you, tap it." Encouraged Shen.

Venkatesh looked at Anna for her opinion, she nodded.

"Very well" Venkatesh took out his tablet, unlocked the screen. "Here goes my life's work." he taped the 'Activate' button. The screen began to show the transfer of last few gigabytes of codes; the transfer was comparatively fast due to the photon based transfer of data that was trademarked under the name Li-Fi. But to them, it appeared to have taken an eternity to reach 99%, and when it did, the tablet screen locked itself and went black. All three of them stared at the Android and were impatiently waiting for the bootup process to finish. There was a death-like silence in the lab in which Venkatesh could almost hear his heart racing. The calmness of their surrounding was in stark contrast to the storm raging in each mind, and in this moment of palpable tension; Isaac woke up.

First, the android raised its head and then slowly opened his eyes. The first thing he saw was Venkatesh's blue shirt; then he moved his head further up to look at Venkatesh's face. He blinked for the first time, then he moved his gaze onto Shen on the right and then Anna on the left. All three of them hunched over, staring at him while Anna's arms shot up in the air.

Chapter 4

"It's alive! It's alive!" Anna announced triumphantly, shooting her arms in the air.

Venkatesh squatted down, eye level to Isaac and smiled, Isaac fixed his gaze on him. Then Venkatesh lifted his right hand and forwarded his open palm towards Isaac. Isaac's gaze quickly shifted to Venkatesh's hand, and he jerked back his upper body abruptly! Venkatesh drew his hand back quickly and looked into Isaac's eyes.

"It's ok; we are not going to harm you, It's okay". Venkatesh slowly moved his hand towards Isaac again. This time, however, Isaac didn't move back, he kept his gaze on Venkatesh, and the Doctor slowly moved his hand closer to Isaac's silicon cheeks and stroked them lightly, Isaac's eye closed and a smile slowly formed on his lips.

"Is he smiling? Oh, look! He is smiling!" Anna stared at Isaac with widened and moist eyes.

"Yes, his tactile feedback is working, the smile is an automated reaction.." This time it was Shen who interrupted Him.

"Don't spoil this moment Doc. I know how it is happening and it's still wonderful!" Shen replied with a broad smile on his face.

"I know. It surely is." Vankatesh kept stroking Isaac's

cheeks lovingly, and a smile crept from Venkatesh's lips to his eyes which were staring back into Isaac's. Then all of a sudden Anna rose an alarm.

" Why isn't it crying? You programmed it like a child, so it should cry. Shouldn't it?" Anna asked worriedly.

"Relax Anna," Venkatesh replied as he turned his head towards Anna and then back to Isaac. "He is smart. He knows that all our attention is focused on him and he doesn't need to do anything to attract it." Venkatesh gently pinched Isaac's cheek. "Don't you? smart little boy."

"Uh, Doc! I have a question. How do you know Isaac is a 'he'? I mean I didn't design any specific parts for him so…" Shen enquired with a shrug of his shoulders while shaking his head. Venkatesh's eyes opened wide as he turned towards Anna.

"I don't, in fact, the only reason I have been referring to Isaac as a male is because his name is 'Isaac'!"

"Don't look at me!" Anna exclaimed crossing her arms. " The only reason I called him Isaac was because it sounded similar to A.I.S.H.A.C and was a better name than that."

"Okay. Nothing to panic!" Venkatesh breathed out heavily. "We will let Isaac figure out with time which gender does he or she wants to identify with when he is capable of processing what genders are, till then we go about calling him Isaac until Isaac want's to get his name changed. Cool?" Venkatesh suggested, gesturing with open palms.

"Wow!, I wish parents in your country were as liberal with their kids as you are." Shen mocked.

"He is not my kid" Venkatesh reminded. "He is an expensive research project, our research project."

"And that reminds me where will Isaac stay tonight?" Anna asked, "Surely we can't leave him in this lab, can we?"

"Of course not!" Venkatesh's jaws dropped. "I programmed him with the psychology of a child; he will cry himself to failure if he finds none to keep him company." Just as Venkatesh had finished and even before he could take a breath, he heard a faint noise of crying. Turning back, they saw Isaac was crying even though his eyes were dry. What they didn't notice was that in between their discussions about Isaac's sex and his nightly accommodation, they had turned their attention completely away from Isaac for quite a while. Isaac processed this by the direction they were looking at and the angle of their body, and this was enough to get him to respond like a human baby would in such a situation. His weeps were slowly getting louder until it got their attention back. Yes! Venkatesh's codes were running smoothly, and he was glad about it. But right now Vankatesh had to go down on his knees to pacify Isaac.

"It's ok! I wasn't annoyed at you; It was Shen and Anna who got me distracted. You have our full attention now." Venkatesh kept on pacifying Isaac as Anna and Shen were giggling behind.

When his crying stopped, Vankatesh got up and told Shen to keep Isaac busy while he was going to to have a drink by the water cooler. He called Anna along with him. Isaac had almost begun to cry a second time seeing Anna and Venkatesh leave, but Shen managed to get his attention focused on himself while they were gone.

#

"I guess I should take Isaac with me tonight." Venkatesh suggested on the way to the water cooler, "That way I will be able to see if he is malfunctioning in any way."

"Ya, like you have any idea how a baby functions that you will know if he is 'malfunctioning'." Anna quipped Venkatesh sarcastically.

"Why does everyone have to bring up my lack of parenting experience in this?" Venkatesh argued. "He is a scientific experiment, I know science, I have written his codes, I know what to expect of him."

" Yes you have written his codes, but you have written them so that he acts like a baby and learn from his experience, didn't you?" Anna asked rhetorically. "And now he is experiencing and adapting to be something different from what you created but he is still a child, and I know his mind because that's what I do."

"I don't doubt your qualifications, but he is not a human kid, You expertise in human psychology. I know about Artificial intelligence." Venkatesh explained while taking a sip of the cold water. " What if you get him home and he starts to behave abnormally, different from an ordinary child like he did when he didn't cry."

"you programmed it to act like a child, and then develop its own sentience with time. Don't you think it will be a problem if it does not act like an average child at this early stage?" Anna asked with concern. "Maybe we should both be together with Isaac tonight, I mean we each have very valid reasons to be with him."

Venkatesh almost coughed up the entire gulp of water he had taken, because of the shock. Anna quickly moved out of the way to dodge the spillage and began stroking Venkatesh on the back to relax his coughing.

"As in we be together in one house?" Vankatesh asked after the coughs subsided. "Are you sure?"

" Hold on to your horses Doctor!" Anna teased him as they started to walk back towards the lab. " You and Isaac will be in one bed, and I will be on the couch."

"Why? Shouldn't you be on the bed and I on the sofa?" Venkatesh asked.

" Oh! That's because in case your programming malfunctions, I don't wanna risk my life." Anna raised her hands in mock deniability.

"Very well, I never thought that I would ever get to ask you this." Venkatesh said coyishly "Your place or mine?"

"Don't you think we should also ask Shen if we are going to have a…" Anna had stopped mid-sentence, surprised by what she saw up ahead when she opened the lab's door to enter. In front of her was Isaac sitting on his chair but clutching the armrest firmly, looking keenly at Shen who was sitting opposite him on a similar chair in the same pose. At this moment Venkatesh who was walking just a few paces behind looked through the ajar door, and his jaws dropped. Shen was slowly and steadily pushing on the armrest and getting up, Issac was mirroring him exactly without any sense of fear or hesitation but keen focus until both Shen and Isaac were facing each other and stood straight up. Vankatesh was admiring the tall and lean-built of the humanoid which had never looked more fantastic till now. Within an hour of his birth. Isaac was on his feet.

Chapter 5

Anna ran in and hugged Shen! Then she quickly turned to Isaac with an ecstatic smile. Isaac smiled back too! First at her and then he turned his head to look at Venkatesh walking in with wide strides as if all the exhaustion of the long day had washed off him. He congratulated Shen and pat his back! Then, turning towards Isaac, took a good look at his creation as he beamed in admiration.

" How did you know! How did you ask him to follow you?" Venkatesh demanded, shaking Shen with excitement and urgency.

"I didn't!" Shen explained. "After both of you had left he was almost brought back to tears. I tried to console him by baby talking to him, but he kept looking at the door as if he wanted to follow you. I thought why not try and see if Isaac could walk, but for that; first, he had to get up, and since you programmed him like a kid, I thought the best way to teach him was to show him.

So I dragged this chair." Shen pointed at the chair right behind him on which he was sitting. "Sat on it, got up and moved towards the door. This caught his attention. I repeated this once more and to my amazement, he was pushing on the floor hard enough to lift his body up in the air! Unfortunately not hard enough to stand up and hence he fell back into the chair. Fearing that he will push too hard and topple over, I sat back on my chair with his focus on me." Shen began to demonstrate by sitting back in his chair. "Then I gripped the armrest rigidly and slowly pushed until I was on my feet and then I straightened up. Isaac followed the exact movements, and here he is, standing; right in front of you. Now we know that the servos are running fine and my simulations were correct."

"I never doubted them!" Venkatesh defended.

"Yes you did, or why else would you make me run them twice?" Shen retorted "Is it because you can't bear my absence from the lab Doc? Awww!"

"Get a room you two, would you?" Anna mocked them. "Focus on the rising star now. Do you think we can teach Isaac to walk now? I mean right now?"

"I don't see why we can't," Venkatesh assured with confidence.

"One little thing that I wanted to ask Doc!" Shen enquired "How is Isaac able to 'focus' I mean it is quite evident that Isaac is fond of you so why would he focus his attention on me when you guys were at the door?"

"That's how I programmed him. Although he gets data from all of his sensors which will be at least in gigabytes, and that's a conservative estimate, but he can choose to process some of that data on a priority basis whereas the other data does get stored for background processing." He Looked at Anna and continued "Isn't that how you said the focus, conscious and subconscious mind work?"

"That's the leading theory," Anna confirmed. "But let us concentrate on the task at hand. Who is going to teach Isaac to take his first step?"

"I would like to do the honour if none of you has any objections," Venkatesh asked in a very eloquent manner and stood up right in front of Isaac. Then he slowly walked to him so that Isaac could watch and process each of his steps. Then he gently took hold of both of Isaac's hand. Braught then forward and held them firmly.

"Wait!" Anna screamed. Everyone turned to her with alarm. "Let me make a video of this. We are not going to miss Isaac's first steps!" She took out her phone, switched on its camera and looking into the screen signalled Venkatesh to go on.

Then Venkatesh turned his head towards Isaac and gave his hand a slight nudge to get his attention. Isaac looked into Venkatesh's eye, his smile never fading and gave a small nod. Then Venkatesh lifted his left leg gently and slowly placed it a step behind his right. Isaac observed this movement and then when Venkatesh gave a slight pull, Isaac lifted his right leg while his hip shifted to the left to balance the weight. He held on to Venkatesh's hand firmly as he cautiously placed his right feet on the solid concrete ground and put his weight on it. Isaac had taken his first step! Anna almost jumped up with joy as slowly Venkatesh kept on walking back and Issac, following his footsteps, walked ahead. Taking one step after the other, his grip on Venkatesh's hand relaxed with each successive step, and he stood up a little straight with each one of them until his grip became so light, that he was practically walking on his own.

It was Christmas in the Lab! Everyone was laughing, hugging and congratulating each other apart from Isaac because he hadn't learned to laugh or speak or embrace yet but that didn't exclude him from being at the receiving end of the hugs. Though it was impossible to tell what was going behind those glassy eyes of his, they assumed that he too was able to feel the joy to some extent as his smile has widened and his ceramic teeth were shining from between the partition of his silicon lips. Shen promised to give his colleagues, including Isaac; a treat of home cooked authentic Chinese food. Venkatesh broke out in a typical Bollywood dance as Anna followed along trying to match his awkward steps.

"Very well! Now my turn to teach Isaac something." Anna suggested enthusiastically. "Observe and learn Isaac!" She too stood straight up in front of Isaac, About an arm's length apart. Pointed at her feet, and Isaac began to observe them keenly. Now she slowly lifted her right leg up, twisted her feet towards the right at her ankle and placed it slowly a few inches away from its previous position. Isaac mirrored the movements with his left feet. Then Anna slowly lifted her left feet in the air, turned her upper body towards her left by 90 degrees and placed her feet straight down such that now she had turned right from her previous position and was facing the door of the lab, as was Isaac. He mirrored each of her movement with perfect accuracy. Now as she took a step forward so did Isaac.

"At this rate, Isaac will be running marathons by the end of this week!" Shen shook his head in disbelief.

"I hate to say this, but he is right." Venkatesh realised at once what he had said and quickly began to explain "I meant that I don't 'hate' to admit that Shen is correct but the implications that it carries. We have done quite a lot of work today, and I think we should call it a night." Shen didn't look too convinced though, but he too was far too tired to argue. "But before we do that, one last thing needs to be done," Venkatesh announced as he walked to the door, held it open and looked at Isaac. "Come on Isaac! I know you can do this." He encouraged Isaac enthusiastically and waved his hands for Isaac to follow him. Isaac, having learned the use of his legs and grown fond of Venkatesh, didn't want to be left behind this time and slowly began to walk towards Venkatesh looking directly ahead at him on Venkatesh's gleaming face. However what he had failed to notice was the creamy cheese left on the floor that had dropped earlier from the Pizza that the team had for dinner that night. Even if he had noticed, he had no way of knowing how slippery a thing can grease be and who could blame him? He was not a day old yet. Till now Venkatesh's team, though aware of the spillage had ignored it and overstepped it every time they went that way. Perhaps they could have got it cleaned had only they not been working so late at night that all the cleaning staff had left.

There's an age-old saying that Venkatesh's father told him when he had failed his English test in 4th standard. "You can't learn to walk without learning to fall." At that time he didn't understand why his father was talking about walking and falling when he could effortlessly run. Later, however, he understood that it was a metaphor for learning from one's failures. Today, however, he was about to learn that it was very literal too. They did notice that Isaac was about to step on the grease. Shen and Venkatesh even ran to stop him. Anna stood dumbstruck fearing the worst and Isaac, he merrily stepped on the cheese without even realising what was waiting for him. Isaac had learned to walk, now he had to learn to fall, and Isaac did fall. Slipping over the cheese when he stepped on it. Alas! He had never experienced a fall or pain, and hence, he did nothing to reduce the impact and fell on his open face and chest. The first sign of damage was the shattered pieces of his ceramic teeth that scattered on the floor and shone like pearls.

Chapter 6

Anna's face was a portrait of agony that only empathy could paint. Empathy is an interesting subject, where one puts oneself in other person's proverbial shoes and imagines what it must feel like to go through the same experience as they are. However, therein lies the flaw. Empathy is involuntary imagination and not actual sensation.

As Isaac lay on the floor, his damage sensors triggered. They were informing his processing unit of all the parts and the different magnitude of injury he had experienced. In human beings, the colloquial term for such sensory impulses is 'pain', and Isaac's programming made sure he processed and reacted to this data in the same way babies dealt with pain. He began to wail.

Venkatesh had reached him by now, and so had Shen. While Venkatesh grabbed on to Isaac's arm, Shen lifted his feet. With both of their coordinated effort, they were able to lift the android's body and place it upright on a nearby chair. Venkatesh shouted Anna's name to pull her out of her trance! Alerted by Venkatesh's call, she rushed towards Isaac and then she saw the extent of the damage. His ceramic teeth had fractured, and the shock had dislodged his lower jaw, the silicone skin had split open at the nose to reveal his broken polymer endoskeleton underneath. His right eye had completely shattered, and the left one had a crack, and this was just the visible injuries. Had Isaac carried any blood, his face would have turned into an unrecognisable bloody mess by now and would have caused Anna to faint perhaps, but all it did in its current state was make her burst into tears. She immediately leaned over and embraced Isaac in her arms and kissed his forehead in an attempt to alleviate his pain. She was succeeding in her efforts as her actions were causing Isaac to lose focus on the damage. The sound of Anna's crying and the wetness of her tears attracted Isaac's attention as these were entirely new things that he observed after his activation. He had never experienced moisture before.

While Anna was trying to pacify Isaac, she too felt a sense of calmness entrapping her. She felt like the dark, cold night had passed. Like the worst was over, when Isaac wrapped his arms around her. Perhaps he was imitating her, as he had till now or maybe it was just because of his programming to form attachments with parent-like figures, or maybe he could feel something, but it didn't matter for her and why would it? What was the essence of this interaction was how she felt about him and how Isaac made Anna feel; for she could never know what was going in his Quantum brain. All she could be aware of was her state of emotions, and Anna was beginning to calm now when all of a sudden, she noticed something frightful. Isaac's wailing had ceased! There was no sound of his breathing! His arms had dropped from her back; his body had gone as limp as it had been before Venkatesh activated him!

Anna immediately pulled herself back to look at Isaac's broken face. Its death like calmness was even more frightening for her than the degree of destruction it had experienced. Her heartbeat shot up again; her throat went dry, the calm she felt moments earlier had proven itself to be the one that precedes every storm, A calmness like death, followed by a tempest of terror.

"Isaac!"Anna shouted as she tried to shake him back to life.

"Calm down Anna. Isaac is not dead. He can't die." Venkatesh was standing right next to Isaac fiddling with his tablet. He stopped for a while when he looked at the bloodshot eyes of Anna filled with fear and anger. "I have put him in a manual sleep mode." He continued to explain to her. "It is akin to medically induced coma in humans. It was built to repair, maintain and update him but I never thought it would be useful so early." If Anna didn't know him for almost half of a decade, she would have mistaken his calmness for lack of emotions, but that is not how Venkatesh worked. He couldn't enjoy the luxury of emotions overpowering him. He had a situation at hand, and he had to deal with it first, maybe after that, he could let his emotions take the best of him, but Anna had no such restraints. It's ironic for someone who knew so well the functioning of other's brain had so little control over her own's. "Why did you make him stop breathing?" The words almost choked her as she tried to fight back another wave of tears.

"He doesn't need to breathe to stay alive, It's just a complementary function to assist his vocal communication,"

Venkatesh explained as he kept on examining the reading of Isaac's damage sensors. "And Shen was the one who built it into him, not me."

"Hey, doc! I heard you two call my name behind my back." Shen came walking in the lab carrying a large toolkit in one hand and a large mug of black coffee in another.

"No time for jokes Shen," Venkatesh warned with the same mechanical calmness as he took the coffee from Shen. " The sensors indicate the impact was on the face and chest, The piezoelectric layer of the skin seems to be damaged as well, and hence the sensors can't be fully trusted. We have to take the skin off to examine him."

"On it doc." Shen took a scalpel from his toolbox and moved towards Isaac.

"Start from the chest please," Venkatesh instructed. Shen stopped to look at Venkatesh first and then at Anna, he gave a slight nod and headed back to his toolkit.

"And as for you Anna! I don't reckon there is much that you can do. I recommend that you go home and take some rest." Venkatesh suggested while examining Isaac's face, Blocking its view from Anna.

"Will you and Shen stay?"Asked Anna timidly.

"We have to. can't leave Isaac alone, not like this." Venkatesh replied before we went back to work. Anna was almost sure she heard him swallowing a lump in his throat.

He wouldn't let his emotions overpower him, not tonight. Anna silently took her bag and walked out as she heard both of her colleagues working on Isaac. Just a few minutes ago, everyone was so cheerful, a long but happy day was about to draw its close at night but now; even as the dawn draws near, there was dark gloominess in her heart, and she was sure of that.

#

She slowly walked her way home, The campus was empty apart from the few guards patrolling the premises, the roads were deserted, and the only audible sound was that of the crickets chirping. Anaa usually had a fast gait, which often became the subject of Venkatesh's joke. He would say she moved so fast cause she wanted to rush into the future. She knew better; it was not to rush into the future, why hasten the inevitable, no! It was to escape from the past, from the guilt that stalked her, that had finally caught up with her. There was no need to run now, no use. She couldn't escape her past, She couldn't escape her guilt for she was never ahead of it; it always accompanied her in her mind, just hidden from the plain view, buried and repressed under forgotten memories and regrets; but existing. Waiting for the right opportunity to leap out of the shadows of past and into the brightness of the present and today, it had. Isaac's fall was just the trigger. His body going limp in her arms was the point-blank shot. When she reached her home, she didn't bother to get a wash or change her clothes, what's the use?

The past clings on. She just lied on the bed exhausted but not because of the long day but because of the long forgotten emotions that flooded her mind. Slowly and gratefully she went to sleep, not because she needed to rest, but because she needed to escape.

Chapter 7

The next morning Anna woke up to the soothing melody of flowing water emitting from the inbuilt speakers in her bed. Her cell phone showed it was 9:00 Am in the morning and that she had 5 hours of disturbed sleep the last night. It also suggested a strong hot espresso with breakfast. Anna tapped the 'yes' button, and the coffee maker jumped into life. After she finished her morning routine, she sat for breakfast and dialled up Venkatesh and Shen, and none of them picked up her call. "They must have fallen asleep in the lab," she thought. " I need to hurry!". She quickly put on a fresh set of T-shirt and trousers, drank the remaining coffee in one go which almost burning her throat, and rushed to the lab.

#

When she had reached there, she found her suspicion to be true. Venkatesh had dozed off on his system which showed no faults in Isaac's codes, much to her relief; and Shen was sleeping on a table beside Issac, using his toolbox as a makeshift pillow. Isaac laid bare of his skin on his face and chest with most of the frontal skeletal structure of his face and eyes removed; It reminded her of the days when Shen was building the robot by custom 3D printed polymer pieces and standard hardware available. At that time Anna had a very active role to play unlike now. After Venkatesh returned from finishing the lectures, she used to teach him about the physiology and psychology of a child's brain and its development so that he could build an analogous model brain for Isaac. In a way, Anna felt Isaac was as much her work as much as it was of the other two because after all, Anna was the one who directed Venkatesh about what to program into Isaac's brain. Isaac's success and failure were as much her responsibility as it was of Shen and Venkatesh and yet here she was looking at a broken robot and unable to help in any way. While she was contemplating her significance to the research, she heard a yawning sound from behind. She turned back to find out that Venkatesh was waking up disturbed by the pale sunlight hitting his face. Even though it visibly bore signs of hard labour and lack of sleep, but it also reflected a serenity of satisfaction. Perhaps the night had truly passed.

" Morning sleepy head!" Anna greeted cheerfully.

"Huh, you are here so early! what time is it?" Venkatesh asked, groggily rubbing his eye.

" Half past nine." Anna checked her watch. " How long had you two been working last night?"

" Guess till 4:30." Venkatesh got off his chair and went towards the door. " Wake up Shen, will you?"

" Ya sure." Anna nodded as she headed to wake Shane up whose saliva had dripped from the edge of his lips onto his toolkit on which his head was resting.

" Yew! Wake up Shane" Anna poked Shen's head with a finger to maintain minimal contact.

" Huh, what!" mumbled a startled Shen. " Oh! It's you, Hi! Good morning!" He greeted while rubbing the sides of his lips and cheek on his shirt's elbow to clean up the saliva.

" Go and clean up Shen!" Scolded Anna. " It's already Half past nine."

" Only? Why wake up so early then?" He was groggy and started to lean back again, but Anna stopped him.

" Go to the restroom and wash up, then go home and sleep all you like" Instructed Anna pulling Shen off the table by his arm.

" Yes, mum!" Shen mocked her as he slowly walked towards the Lab's exit. Just when he was about to exit, Venkatesh entered with his hair wet and combed up neatly, A little wakeful than he was when he had left.

" Freshen up and go home, Shen." Suggested Venkatesh " Have some sleep and see you in the evening."

" Why freshen up when one has to go back to sleep again?" Shen complained as he slowly made his way towards the restroom.

" You had any breakfast, Anna?" Venkatesh asked.

" Ya, before I came here" Anna answered.

" Good for you cause I am famished. Care to join?" Venkatesh offered. "I gotta talk to you about something."

Anna nodded and walked out of the lab as Venkatesh

locked the biometric lock and they slowly walked towards the nearest canteen.

" So how is Isaac's now?" Anna enquired.

" Oh better than we thought." Venkatesh consoled her. " His electronics were almost intact. Shen repaired the little damage they had incurred. The codes are running perfectly now. The pneumatic muscles and fibre skeleton absorbed most of the shock, so that's comforting. The face needs to be replaced. Without much covering, it took the maximum amount of damage. I will order the parts today itself. Filing the paperwork for funding will be a pain though."

" Oh, that's good news!" Exclaimed Anna.

"Indeed that is, but everything is not," Venkatesh commented while staring at her. " Sit, I will order first and then explain." He went to the reception to place an order then came back and took a seat opposite Anna.

" Do you know why we designed the robotic shell for Isaac as a humanoid?" Venkatesh asked her.

" Yes! So that he could sense the world like a human does. Didn't you?" Anna questioned back.

" Indeed. But there lies the problem, The Uncanny valley. Something that's not entirely human and yet resembles a human." Venkatesh explained, " And last night your reaction to the accident made me feel like you are too emotionally involved with Isaac!"

" No! I am not! I mean he is my project too." Anna defended. " After the last night's accident, I was afraid that he might be damaged. What's wrong with that, isn't it natural?"

" Were you anxious that it may have been damaged or were you worried that he might be hurt?" Venkatesh frowned while staring sharply into Anna's eye; she looked away. " You were afraid that he had died in your arms when I put him in manual sleep mode. didn't you?"

" I don't know what are you are talking about; I remember no such thing." Anna tried to dodge Venkatesh's suspicion." You must be tired and delusional. You need to sleep."

" And you need to wake up," Venkatesh warned. " You were holding him in your arms and crying."

" Yes, I was! Maybe because I am not as cold-hearted as you are." Anna yelled all of a sudden! Then she looked around to see people quickly turning their gazes away from her. So she lowered her volume and continued angrily. "Maybe nothing bothers you because you feel no pain for anyone. Nor for those people involved in the Turing fiasco, neither for Isaac. He is just a project for you, isn't he? But he is much more for me, Dr Vankateshwara Iyer." Anna was uncontrollably yelling again and had attracted the attention of everyone in the canteen. All pair of eyes were fixed on them, and Venkatesh looked around, and everyone turned back, as his gaze met theirs. He got up to leave, but before he did, he turned towards Anna with his now sunken but enraged eyes.

" I know he means a lot to you but understand well that he is not a human, not yet!" Venkatesh punched the table. "Maybe someday he will be or maybe not. That's the experiment, and sometimes experiments fail. Take my word for it." He paid the bill at the counter and left. He headed towards the parking lot where he had left his bicycle and was about to ride away when he saw Anna standing in front of him.

" I am sorry Venkatesh! " Anna apologised " I shouldn't have talked to you like that."

" No you shouldn't, but what could you do? I was right about you, and the truth hurts. Doesn't it? Venkatesh retorted as he rode away toward his apartment.

Chapter 8

That day Shen woke up again at 2:00 PM and found himself on his comfortable single bed. For a moment he was tempted to go back to sleep, but then he realised he had not eaten anything since the last night when he had that Pizza. The realisation filled him with regret for his hurry to pick up the slice which led to the accident. He felt responsible for the damage to Isaac's body and the extra work that Venkatesh had to put in to salvage the situation. He also noticed Anna's bloodshot eyes and her tear marks when she left the lab the night before, and the guilt engulfed him. Although the situation was under control now, he had to do something to make up for his mistake, but what? He was contemplating his repentance while brushing his teeth in front of the mirror when he heard the familiar sound of his rumbling stomach. " Boy! If only I had eaten something earlier I could think better" He thought to himself as he spat out the paste when suddenly an idea struck him " I know! I will prepare a home cooked meal for them. I had already promised them dinner last night, let's make that happen tonight!" With a newly found enthusiasm, he finished up brushing his teeth and began to look through his mom's cooking notes. Selected a few classics including Gong Bao chicken and Ma Po Tofu and ordered the ingredients online. Looking at his watch, he found it has already been 3: 00 PM and concluded that most likely Venkatesh would be napping, so he called Anna.

" Hey Anna, calling to check on you, Would you be free tonight for dinner? I am cooking home cooked Chinese dinner for the three of us.".

" Yes, Shen! I would love to, but have you confirmed with Venkatesh if he would join in?" Anna hesitated.

" Not yet. The Doc would be taking a nap right now, but I have included vegetarian on the menu as well." Shen assured, double checking his grocery list. Venkatesh had almost habituated Shen to his ritual of double checking things.

" Not that!" Anna said unsurely " You leave it. Call Venkatesh when he wakes up."

" Wait a minute. What do you mean by 'not that'?" Shen's eyes narrowed in suspicion. " what happened?"

" He is a little angry at me since we had a verbal spat in the morning at the canteen and I may have casually mentioned the Turing thing." Anna explained while clenching her teeth " You know how childish grudges he can hold when he is angry, don't you?"

" Why would you do that?" Shen asked in exasperation " You know how sensitive he becomes when the Turing incident comes up, particularly when people surround him."

" I know! I am sorry, I ran after him to apologise, and yet he turned his back on me" she said apologetically " He was interrogating me about how much I care for Isaac and why I shouldn't and I …"

" It's ok; I can understand he can be a little pushy sometimes." Shen consoled her. " But his intentions are good; he doesn't want you to be hurt the same way the others were."

" What else do you think I apologised to him for." Anna retorted.

" Hey! Cool it down lady don't snap at me." Shen appealed. " I am going to cook Chicken for you."

" Oh! I am sorry again! Do you think you can convince him to stop acting up?" Anna pleaded.

" Maybe! But I definitely can't take the risk of calling you two together." Shen mentioned when the doorbell rang, and his cell phone issued a vibration alert. " Ya talk to you later, I guess the delivery drone is at the door. Chao." And indeed the delivery drone was hovering just a few feet away from Shen's front door; It was wi-fi enabled to connect to Shen's doorbell and cell phone. Shen took the package off it, swiped his grocery retail membership card, and the drone flew away after wishing him a good day. As soon as it had left, he began to order another set of edibles to execute his new plans. At about 5 in the evening, he called Venkatesh.

" Hey, Doc! What are you doing?" Shen asked casually

" Just waking up from a peaceful nap." Yawned Venkatesh " Why?"

" Just wondering if I may interest you with a games

night." Shen proposed " There will be food, Strictly veg, beer and video games, You in?"

" Tonight?"

" Yes, What better night than this evening? We are going to be busy from tomorrow again aren't we?" Shen mentioned.

" Yes, we will be," Venkatesh affirmed. " They called in to inform the parts will be delivered by tomorrow. Okay, count me in."

" Cool, See you in one hour?"

" Ya sure, I'll be there," Venkatesh affirmed. " Uhh, listen, will Anaa be there too?"

" Unless she has suddenly developed an interest in games or pure vegetarian food, I don't see the point in inviting her." Shen reasoned.

" Ya, sure! Why would the lady be interested in such lowly pursuits?" Venkatesh mumbled " See you later then, Bye!"

#

Later in the evening when Shen and Venkatesh were sipping on their cans of cold beer while slaughtering virtual zombie hoards in immersive virtual reality, Shen casually brought up the topic of Anna. " Everything fine between you and Anna?"

Venkatesh looked at Shen's avatar in the V.R a little startled, but gained his composure and went on cracking an undead's skull open. " Ya, everything is fine, Why do you ask?"

"Nothing! Just being silly." Shen casually dodged the question. " To your right Doc!"

Venkatesh turned to his right to find a 'Chernie'. A physically enhanced undead infused with radioactive isotopes. They were called Chernie in reference to the Chernobyl disaster. Venkatesh selected the shotgun from his arsenal and quickly blew up the Chernie's head. "Thanks!" Venkatesh thanked Shen for his timely warning, and they fist bumped to celebrate. " Head on to the next checkpoint," Venkatesh instructed.

After both of them had reached the next checkpoint safely, Venkatesh began. "Shen, do you think it is all right to invest in Isaac emotionally?" Venkatesh asked, " Don't you think one might lose perspective?"

"Oh! Absolutely Doc!" Shen nodded " Isaac is uncharted territory, we can't treat him like a normal human and get blinded by emotions. If only those scientist had terminated their research at earlier stages, there wouldn't be a zombie viral outbreak."

" Exactly! I mean why treat him like a kid when he is not. I know he is programmed to behave like one but what if the experiment fails and he becomes unable to feel any emotions at all." Venkatesh explained while sawing an undead's brain into two.

" Ya, that would be like loving a piece of technology which wouldn't be bound to follow your orders or love you back," Shen affirmed after shooting a zombie in the eye and chugging down his beer in one sip. " I wouldn't tolerate if my cell phone started to act up. Tough love it would be for it then."

" Now If only Anna could understand that." Venkatesh lamented as he had to finish off a member of his troop who was bitten by a zombie hiding under a blown up car. " Rest in peace mate!"

" I am sure Anna could understand if you will explain it to her properly. She is intelligent enough." Shen assured.

" No doubt she is, but she is emotional too. Can't see the problem with A.I," Venkatesh continued. " I mean, consider private Jenkins. He was as good as dead the moment he was bitten, not killing him off would have only prolonged his agony and the threat to our squad."

" Hear my friends, for the truth, has been spoken," Shen announced to his virtual team members who were staring down at Private Jenkins burning corpse. Both of them were about to move on ahead with the game when suddenly the game went into auto-pause with a notification of someone being at the door. Shen took off his VR headset and stood up from his couch to receive the new guest and Venkatesh extended his arm to unlock the door as he was sitting close to it. On the other side, was Anna.

"Oh! Welcome Anna, and I thought you would never have joined us." Shen welcomed her. Venkatesh took off his V.R headset and was surprised to see her. "Oh hi! I didn't know you were coming, coincidentally we were talking about you now. We have lost a man to a zombie, think you can replace him?"

"What did he drink?"Anna leaned towards Shen while staring suspiciously at Venkatesh.

"A can of chilled beer, followed by chilled vodka mixed with soda, in a can of beer" Shen gave her a mischievous smile.

"He didn't notice?"

"What do you think the game and the first can of beer was for ?" Shen jibed. "Now you go, and bond over some undead corpses and I will prepare the dinner."

"Oh come on Shen! We are already a man down." Venkatesh protested.

"And I am sure the lady will make up for my absence, Just teach her the controls. I have to prepare dinner to retain our strengths Doc." Shen excused before going into the kitchen, and Anna sat beside Venkatesh.

"Ok! Here is how you do it." He handed her the remote and began to explain the controls. "When you put on the headset you will see a holographic bracelet around your wrist from which you can choose your weapons. Your health and ammunition gauges are on your display. To walk, jump and run you just got to think about it and the electrodes will pick up the brain waves. Follow my lead, and you shall stay alive. So; shall we begin?"

Anna put on the headset and gave the nod, and Venkatesh unpaused the game.After slaughtering a few dozens of zombies together and managing to survive to the end of the current stage, Venkatesh apologised to Anna. "I am sorry to behave so rudely to you. It's just that I care about you and don't want you to hurt the same way as those who were left heartbroken after the truth about project Turing came about on national television."

" It's all right Venkatesh. I am an adult, and I can take care of myself and my emotions, and don't worry! I was hurt worse than anything you can imagine when I miscarried five months into a pregnancy."

"Oh! I am sorry!" Venkatesh vision blurred, and stomach churned " I didn't know or else I would not have.."

"It's ok Venkatesh; I know you wouldn't have hurt me if you knew." Anna consoled him while checking her ammunition."The thing is no matter however you try you can't stop the pain forever and you shouldn't. Not just it saves you from damaging yourself, but it means you are alive. To live is to suffer, and to be conscious is to be in agony; for nothing bothers the dead. Case in point, these wretched undead hoards. They don't feel any pain, love, regret, longing, nothing. Why live like them when you are alive?"

Venkatesh kept looking at her with a newfound admiration, it's fine to be highly intelligent and qualified, but it is legendary to bond over undead corpses in a post-apocalyptic world. Venkatesh quickly switched his shotgun to chainsaw as the countdown to the next level started. "Oh! Zombies will feel pain; because today, I will make them feel it." He clenched his teeth as they both ran together into the oncoming horde.

A few hours and zombie massacres later, Shen announced to everyone's delight "Dinner is served."

Chapter 9

Shen had to put in twice the effort that night to cook pure vegetarian dishes for Venkatesh and chicken and duck for himself and Anna, but he considered it a worthy investment considering how well were they bonding over food, and Venkatesh was considerate enough not to puke Shen's efforts down the drain. After they had finished, Anna decided that Venkatesh was too drunk to ride back home and hence he should stay back at Shen's and leave early in the morning for his apartment. Venkatesh happily obliged by dozing off on the couch even before Anna could ask him to.

" He looks like a kid doesn't he, So peaceful and placid." Anna observed.

" With alcohol in blood and food in the tummy, everyone will be peaceful as a sleeping baby," Shen remarked while looking at Venkatesh.

Anna giggled at Shen's remark. " Very well then, thanks for the food and company, see you in the morning."

"Wait, do you want me to walk you to your home?" Shen offered chivalrously.

" Thanks for the offer but in case you forget, you too are drunk and fed," Anna reminded him. " Go to sleep Shen; I can walk back to my place."

" Talk about dying chivalry," Shen bid her farewell and

closed the doors behind her, Put the dishes in the washer and went off to sleep.

#

The next day Venkatesh left early at 6 for his home to freshen up. All the three of them were at the lab by half-past 9; The supplier was scheduled to deliver the replacement parts today.

" Anna could you; please Prepare the silicone solution to cast Isaac's face, Shen knows the where about of the mould I believe," Venkatesh instructed Anna.

"On it" Anna affirmed.

"Shen, I have been trying to call professor Anatsui of the fine arts department, she isn't picking up the call," Venkatesh informed. " Could you please request her in person to come a couple of hours later to paint the silicone mask into a face."

" A lady is not picking up your call, so that's what they call a déjà vu." Shen jibed.

" Okay, all that is left is to print the frontal part of the skull and jaws for Isaac." Venkatesh murmured to himself. Then we went to Shen's workstation. " Shen, In which folder do you keep the designs of the skeletal frame of Isaac?"

"Oh God! The printer ran out of the ABS filament." Shen complained. " shall I order it?"

"It's ok, I shall borrow some from some other department, The whole Institute must not have run out of printer filaments, let me make a few calls," Venkatesh assured, and after making a few calls, Venkatesh left.

By the time Shen returned he had found that Anna had already finished with the casting and was correcting Answers sheets of her students. Shen was closely followed by a tall, dark-skinned lady carrying a large backpack. She was in her early twenties. Wearing a sleeveless top and skirts. Sporting shoulder-length Black hair coloured with red and yellow fiery stripes at the ends. White canvas shoes with ankle length socks gave her gait the stealth of a cat.

"Apparently Professor Anatsui has left for a conference in Ghana, but her daughter, Ms Oleta Anatsui have volunteered for our cause and from what I hear she is the best in her class." Shen introduced the Lady.

"They said so because of the inherent nepotism in our system and the mediocrity of standards of fine arts in this institution." Oleta clarified gloomily.

"That's quite the spirit, Ms Oleta!" Anna remarked sarcastically.

"Positivity does not change the depressing truth of our existence, Dr Ainsworth. I am hopeful that you realise that." She mentioned softly.

" Well, that is debatable, but for now there is your

proverbial canvas." Anna pointed to the silicone casting of Isaac's face. " Bring it to life, will you?"

"Why? So that it can go through all the miseries of existence?" Oleta inquired with an air of dejection. " I will do it. Do you have any reference to how would you like it to look?"

" I can help with that." Anna took out her cell to show her the photos of Isaac before he was activated.

"The images look like the work of an amateur. But I can make do with it." She said in a disappointed manner as she placed her backpack on the table on which Isaac's face was drying. She took out her painting kit and tools, put on her earphones and sat to work.

" Where did you pick up this depressed soul form?" Anna whispered to Shen turning her back towards Oleta.

"She had good reviews online. " Shen retorted. "You want me to return her."

" Are you serious?"Anna asked with a frown.

" Not me but she is," Shen commented looking at Oleta. "Like I.C.U serious."

A few hours later Venkatesh returned with a pool of black ABS filament with his shirt drenched in sweat and breathing heavily.

" Looks like you had to fight someone to bring the filament Doc." Shen took the pool from him and went on to place it on the printer. Anna offered him a water bottle. After Venkatesh had drunk adequately from it, he explained. " I had a flat tire. Had to drag my cycle from the Design and production department, In times like this does one wonder why do we have such a big campus? How far did you guys get?

" Professor Anatsui is out of the country, so we have a substitute artist, her daughter Oleta Anatsui." Anna pointed towards Oleta working in the corner. " Trust me you wouldn't want to meet her."

" Why? Do you know anything about her?" Venkatesh looked at Anna in surprise. " She is the literal definition of brilliance. She has been recently offered an internship at Glasgow School of Arts. Her mothers say she is even more talented than her."

"Really?" Anna inquired doubtfully Staring at Oleta" Who informed you?"

"Her mother, of course, Professor Anatsui." Replied Venkatesh as he picked up his cell from his pocket and went outside to talk. He came back a few minutes later with a large parcel in his hand which he kept on his table. He called Shen to inform him that the parts have arrived.

"And the parts will be printed in about an hour, Cleaning and polishing might take about half an hour max, and then we can begin the assembly." Shen informed, "How much time do you think you will need Ms Oleta?"

"It's done, To the best of my uninspiring talent," Oleta replied, unplugging her earphones from her cell.

"Did you guys say something?" Venkatesh asked suspiciously looking back and forth at Shen and Oleta.

"Ya Doc. We welcomed her." Shen replied as Venkatesh was left scratching his head.

As the three of them headed to take a closer look at Oleta's work, they stood dumbfounded in their way. In front of them was the most lifelike silicone face they could not even dream of, Venkatesh moved towards her to take a closer look when he noticed the beautifully sculpted delicate veins and freckles on Isaac's face. The lips were the perfect shade of pink as if supplied with fresh blood; The cheeks had a slight tinge of blush. Moreover, Oleta had punched the hair in the silicone to create real looking eyebrows and eyelashes for Isaac. Even Anna couldn't resist from giving her a literal Standing ovation.

'Wow' was all that Shen could utter.

"Literal brilliance!"Venkatesh quoted.

"I am glad that I don't have to do it over," Oleta said in relief.

Everyone turned to look at her with disbelief. Here was a person blessed with immense talent and yet not even the admiration of her work could bring a smile to her face. Was this just an act? Or was she that depressed, and how can someone so dead inside make something so lively? In between the three of them, they had a combined I.Q of 400, and even they couldn't figure out this mystery.

"Would you like to join us for lunch Ms Oleta?"Venkatesh invited her after checking his watch.

Shen and Anna stared at Venkatesh with wide eyes.

"Ya, that's the least we could do to thank you" Venkatesh cast a glance toward his teammates.

"Ya, I guess that is the least even you can do Doctor, and even I am compelled by my biological need to eat."

"Lunch with you would be so much fun that I can barely wait,"Anna replied sarcastically while Shen just gritted his teeth.

"Life is wasted in waiting. Let's go to whichever sub standard establishment you guys prefer to." Oleta zipped her bag as she headed with them.

Chapter 10

Venkatesh and his company took Oleta to their favourite eatery on the campus, It wasn't an expensive place but the food was good and the ambience peaceful. Oleta was sitting beside Anna and opposite Shen. Venkatesh began to take their orders. After Shen and Anna came Oleta's turn.

" My choice doesn't matter; Food is for nourishment, it would suffice if it serves the purpose, I trust your knowledge on that matter Dr Venkatesh" Oleta replied. Venkatesh moved away to the reception without a second question, Shen, however, wasn't going to endure any more disdain for food.

" Ms Oleta! what have you lost in your life to be so gloomy, apart from a sense of gratitude for the good stuff that you have," Shen asked with annoyance in his voice.

"What good things are you talking about?" Oleta asked curiously. Shen took in a deep breath before replying, A satisfied smile formed on his face.

"Why! The food, of course, one of the greatest gifts that the gods have bestowed upon us mere mortals" Shen explained eloquently.

"Oh, you mean the same food that is doused in a generous amount of carcinogenic chemicals?" Oleta confirmed.

"Ah! So organic farming is your deal." Shen exclaimed with a sense of epiphany.

"No! I don't believe in such luxury." Oleta continued, seeing the confused look on Shen's face " The resources consumed to grow vegetables organically is wasteful at best. It's like using mineral water to bathe your canine companion."

" Well, if everything that you eat is going to either kill you or the earth then I would gladly die gluttoning on extra cheese with a generous scoop of cancer." Shen declared.

" Oh! You don't need to worry about Cancer." Oleta assured. " By the choice and portion of your order, it is apparent that obesity and diabetes will take you down long before cancer arrives."

" Oh stop it you two," Anna intervened. " We don't talk about who is going to die of what at lunch."

"Oh, Pardon me Dr Anna, but when do you speak of death then?" Oleta inquired with curiosity.

" We usually don't Ms Oleta," Anna explained with surprise. " Not since we have known each other."

" Ah! Ignorance is truly blissful I assume." Oleta concluded with a heavy sigh.

"Indeed it is, I wish we could have ignored you back in the lab, It would have to been so…" Shen was interrupted by Venkatesh before he could finish his witty jibe.

"Hey Shen, Behave! She is our guest" Venkatesh reminded Shen as he placed the heavy tray containing all their orders on the table. Then he sat down on a chair, Handled a plate of pasta to Oleta and asked her if it would suffice.

" Indeed it will Dr Venkatesh," Oleta assured. " It is more than what some people get to eat in a whole day in certain parts of the world."

"Oh no, we can order more for you, I assure you we have no shortage." Venkatesh persuaded her.

" Yes! We will die of excess." Oleta concluded.

"Are you not glad that she joined us for lunch Doc!" Shen asked Venkatesh sarcastically.

" I have forgotten what gladness feels like," Venkatesh whispered back.

For the next half an hour, all four of them had their lunch with an awkward silence. After the group had done, they walked Oleta out of the eatery where they parted from Oleta to go their separate ways.

" Thanks for paying for my food Dr Venkatesh. I am relieved to know my efforts can earn me lunch at least" Oleta expressed her gratitude before leaving.

" It is worth lot more Ms Oleta," Assured Venkatesh as they left. When they had walked a considerable distance away from Oleta's presumably hearing range, Shen turned to Venkatesh.

" What were you thinking inviting her with us," Shen asked in vexation.

" Don't you think she was interesting, I mean why she is so grim." Venkatesh wondered looking back in Oleta's direction.

" Apparently because others around her are not." Shen jibed.

" I don't think she is sadistic but rather a nihilist." Venkatesh theorised.

" And you thought that you would be able to figure out her backstory over lunch." Anna mocked him "Didn't you Dr Venkateshwara Iyer?"

" Why wouldn't she be gloomy?" Shen asked in surprise. " She doesn't appreciate food! If a plate full of pasta with white sauce can't bring a smile on your face, then nothing can."

" Shut up Shen, she is a great artist who has done her job, and we still have our's to do." Venkatesh reminded them as they hurried along to their lab.

#

By the time they had reached the lab, the 3D printer had finished its job, Shen had gone to add the finishing touches, Venkatesh had begun to fit the new cameras in Isaac's eye socket, and Anna started to cut the piezoelectric artificial skin into shape and solder the wires protruding from the edges. After about a couple of hours of work, Isaac was back again to his prime conditions.

"He looks more lively than ever, doesn't he?" Anna asked in admiration.

" With all credit to you know who," Venkatesh commented, nudging Shen with his shoulders.

"Vanity came after fall." Shen quoted. " The real work is still mine Doc!"

"And no one denies that, so shall we begin?" asked Venkatesh unlocking his tablet and forwarding it towards Anna.

Anna affirmed as she deactivated the manual sleep override. Isaac's mind started to get the current data regarding the present state of his parts from all over his body. There was no pain this time. Isaac woke up again as a child had awakened after a peaceful sleep.

" Good evening Isaac. It's a pleasure to see you again."Venkatesh greeted with an enthusiastic smile. The next thing Isaac did make their heart skip a beat and eyes wet. Isaac slowly parted his new lips for the first time but not to smile, but to do something that made Venkatesh and his team smile from ear to ear.

" Iaac" Was the first word that Isaac spoke.

" Oh my goodness! Isaac's speaks" Shen Exclaimed!

" I know he did, didn't he? You heard it too right." Venkatesh looked at them in disbelief.

"Of Course I did, every one of us did!' Exclaimed Anna as she jumped with joy.

" All right guys, Take it slow, Remember the last time." Venkatesh warned, "We don't want him to cut his tongue off this time."

" Oh! Don't be such a killjoy Doc!' Shen rolled his eyes. Anna however slowly went down on her knees in front of Isaac and slowly repeated his name " I-saac."

Isaac tried to repeat continuously. " Iyaak."

"Iyaak."

"Iyaak"

"Ishyak"

"Ishyak"

"Izaak"

"Izaak"

"isaac"

"Isaac" Finally Isaac pronounced his name correctly after multiple attempts.

Chapter II

"Yes! Yes! He did it! He did it!" Anna exclaimed in triumph, hugging Isaac. "Good boy Isaac, good lad!"

"I thought his first words would be mama or dada."Shen contemplated.

"Not really. Issac is just mimicking what he hears and how he sees the words pronounced, names are the most repetitive." Venkatesh explained looking at an ecstatic Anna.

"You don't say!"Shen quickly kneeled down in front of Isaac and pronounced his name slowly while baring his teeth and parting his lips apart. Isaac copied the movement of Shen's lips and teeth and pronounced Shen's name almost correctly in his first attempt. "Shhane."

Shen jumped up on his feet with excitement. "Hell Ya! Way to go buddy!" Shen lifted up his palm expecting a high five from Isaac, but all he did was stare at Shen's open palm and lift up his own in imitation. Shen had to make do with lightly tapping Isaac's palm while Isaac watched curiously.

"Ok, my turn now! get up Shen" Anna demanded while rapidly patting Shen's back to get him to hurry, then she took his position in front of Isaac.

"Ok Isaac, say Anna" Anna slowly pronounced her name biting her tongue lightly to show Isaac how to make the 'nna' sound.

Isaac imitated the movements "An-a". He kept on repeating it trying various positions with his tongue as Anna demonstrated with her own until he was capable of pronouncing her name too.

"That's my boy!"Anna Praised Isaac as she stroked his hair with affection, Isaac bent his head forward to welcome her."Awww! You like this, don't you?"

"Anna," Isaac said with a smile.

"Wait!"Venkatesh exclaimed with excitement. "Did you guys see that? do you guys realise what just happened?"

"Ya Doc! Isaac likes when Anna strokes his hair."Shen mentioned casually "Obvious, considering his programming, isn't it?"

"Ya that is evident, but he repeated her name, That's positive reinforcement. Isaac thinks he will be rewarded if he takes her name correctly. His this behaviour can be used to train him." Venkatesh explained.

"What do you mean train him, Venkatesh?"Anna looked offended "He is not your pet."

"I didn't mean that"Venkatesh explained. "But pets are intelligent too, Just saying."

"But what now Doc?" Shen intervened to dilute the tension. "I mean what do we do now that Isaac has learned to speak?"

"Oh, he hasn't learned to speak." Anna explained, "He is

just learning to pronounce different sounds yet, I don't think he still has started to associate meaning with them."

"Exactly! that is going to take time," Venkatesh assured. "Meanwhile we train.." Venkatesh corrected mid-sentence when he realised that Anna was staring at him with anguish. " I said 'teach'. Meanwhile, we teach him how to pronounce different syllables."

"We get to baby talk to him?"Anna asked googly-eyed.

"I don't think that would be necessary, he is capable of learning standard speech quite effectively," Venkatesh informed.

"No wonder you are still single Doc!" Shen muttered under his breath.

"What was that?"Venkatesh inquired suspiciously.

" Nothing Doc! So how do you suggest we teach him?" Shen asked changing the subject.

"Oh! I guess Anna will be able to tell us that. She is the child psychologist." Venkatesh reminded.

"Well usually babies learn by baby talk, but since that won't be necessary, I suggest that we describe our regular activities and objects my their name to Issac. That way he will be able to associate sounds with meaning, and that is what spoken language essentially is."

"Ok! That way he would understand us but how would he learn to speak?" Shen inquired.

"The same way he learned to speak our names, by practising the pronunciations," Anna suggested. "But on the mention of names, Isaac has not yet uttered your name, Venkatesh."

"Seriously? You guys want to be stuck here until the morning?"Venkatesh looked at them over his spectacle's rim as both Shen and Anna burst out laughing. Isaac was smiling as he looked at them.

"And that reminds me the critical issue of Isaac's nightly accommodation," Anna recalled the conversation they were having before Isaac had learned to stand up on his feet and walk. "Which place are we gonna stay in, Yours or mine?"

Venkatesh was blushing bright red at the mention of him and Anna sharing an apartment. Shen was looking confused at what was transpiring.

"His or yours, as in?" Shen asked Anna, staring back and forth at her and Venkatesh.

"As in, his or mine apartment. We both decided that Isaac needs to stay with both of us so that we could monitor him." Anna explained.

"Oh ho ho! Damn this is your lucky day Doc!" Shen giggled as he nudged Venkatesh with his shoulder.

"Of course one of us will be sleeping beside Isaac while the other one will be on the couch."Anna clarified shyly.

" For now I bet!" Shen replied with a mischievous grin.

"Let's not behave like teenagers if you may." Venkatesh intervened "In the earlier stages Isaac needs to be monitored by both of us for obvious reasons, and since he can't be left alone, we need to take him home with us." Then he turned to Anna "That being said it would be preferable to stay in your apartment as mine and Shen's are a bachelor's pad; if you know what I mean."

"Very well! It is decided then. *Me casa es su casa*." Anna affirmed. "Let me call the cab then, I am not going to risk Isaac walking all the way to my place."

"Ya, I will get my cycle, You two can go in the cab," Venkatesh suggested pointing at Anna and Isaac as he began to walk out of the lab.

Shen headed toward Isaac. " Very well Isaac, time to get up." Shen took hold of Isaac's hands and gave them a little nudge upward, but Isaac quickly pulled his hands back. The smile on his lips faded.

" Isaac, are you all right?" Shen looked at Isaac with alarm. "Get up boy! Time to go home". Shen again tried to hold his hands, but Isaac quickly retracted them backwards. Isaac's eyes had widened, and breathing was heavy as he kept staring at the floor. For the first time, Shen saw fear in Isaac's eyes.

" Doc!" Shen screamed in alarm as he ran outside to call Venkatesh. Startled by Shen's scream Anna too ran outside to meet Shen. She saw that Shen was running back towards the lab closely followed by Venkatesh. She turned back to a familiar sound of crying. Isaac was sobbing while staring towards her. Anna immediately ran to pacify him as Venkatesh and Shen entered.

" What happened?" Venkatesh demanded, out of breath.

" I don't know, Shen screamed and ran away, I ran to check on him when Isaac began to weep," Anna informed.

" Isaac is refusing to get up!" Shen stuttered as he broke the devastating news. "I think he is scared of walking."

Chapter 12

"How is that possible?" Venkatesh's jaws dropped. "I didn't programme him to be afraid."

"But you programmed him to detect damage and preserve himself, didn't you?" Anna reminded him. "He is trying to prevent damage to himself by falling. That's fear." Anna kept on stroking Isaac's cheeks and hair to comfort him while Shen and Venkatesh checked the feed from the sensors in Isaac's legs.

"I don't understand. Isaac's legs are fine; his pneumatic muscles are working perfectly even his damage sensors are silent." Venkatesh tried to contemplate the obvious. " Can Isaac be really frightened?"

" What do we do now Doc!, I mean both of us together can lift him up and put him in the car," Shen suggested.

" Have you gone mad?" Anna yelled at him. " Do you know what will that do to him? Do you think he will ever be able to trust any of us ever again?"

" I am sorry!" Shen apologised. " I didn't mean that. I meant maybe we could put him to manual sleep override as we did before until we figure out what's wrong."

"Seriously!" Anna asked in exasperation. " That's your solution? To put him to sleep and carry him like a dead body? How difficult is it for you two to understand that Isaac is showing all the classic signs of basophobia. He is afraid that if he tries to walk, he may fall and hurt himself."

"I have to assume for now that her hypothesis is correct." Venkatesh looked up from his tablet's screen "There is nothing wrong with his body so most likely the problem is in his mind. It looks like we have to stay in the lab until we figure this one out."

"Or we can get a wheelchair for Isaac,"Anna suggested.

"That's a brilliant idea; we can go to the Health centre to borrow a wheelchair, Can't we Doc!" Shen asked

"Indeed we can, Has the cab arrived yet?" Venkatesh asked Anna.

"Yes! The location shows it's here." Anna affirmed "Ya, got the confirmation message too. It's waiting outside."

"Very well Anna, you keep Isaac company," Vankatesh instructed. "Shen! you come with me."

"I have forwarded you the OTP for the ride," Anna informed Venkatesh as he left for the automated cab which was waiting outside the lab. As they got in Venkatesh instructed the cab A.I to change the destination from Anna's home to the institution's Health centre and dialled in the OTP. The electrically powered cab trotted away silently in the night. Venkatesh had paid the cab beforehand so that as soon as the cab arrived at the destination, they rushed into the Health centre without waiting for the taxi's A.I to ask for a review or delivering the polite greeting.

#

"Shen! Call the other cab for the lab; this shouldn't take time"Venkatesh instructed as he ran in towards the reception. "Excuse me, Miss! Could you tell me where can I borrow a wheelchair from?" He asked the young receptionist. She politely pointed him towards the ward boy's cabin. "Thank you."

Venkatesh walked down the hallway to find the ward boy's cabin, but to his dismay, it was locked from the outside. He walked back to the receptionist to inform of the situation to which she consoled him that the guy must have gone to the toilet and he will return soon.

"Ya Doc! The cab is confirmed and it will arrive shortly" Shen informed.

"I wish you would have said that about the ward boy," Venkatesh mumbled pacing up and down the hall impatiently, It had been ten minutes since they had arrived. Running out of patience, he walked back to the receptionist to ask for any possible contact number for the ward boy, Just then to Venkatesh's relief the receptionist pointed out toward a lean frame walking in towards the reception from outside. He was apparently the ward boy for whomVenkatesh was waiting.

"Excuse me! I need to borrow a wheelchair, what's the procedure." Venkatesh asked the ward boy as soon as he entered the premises.

"It doesn't look like you need a wheelchair." Commented the lean figure while looking at Venkatesh's feet and chewing what suspiciously looked like tobacco.

"Not for me but for someone I know."Venkatesh clarified as he walked hurriedly alongside the guy toward his cabin.

"Who? You need to get a doctor's recommendation to borrow the wheelchair." The ward boy informed while unlocking the door to his cabin.

"Look Mr P Pandey." Venkatesh noticed the name sewn in on his uniform. "I need the wheelchair for my project. A damaged robot, a mechanical humanoid. Doctors don't treat them, scientists and engineers do."

"Sorry, Mr Scientist." P.Pandey continued after spitting the tobacco in a dustbin. "Can't lend you a wheelchair until you get it written by a doctor on duty."

"Very well Mr P Pandey, Listen carefully!" Venkatesh rolled up his sleeves as he stared down at the guy." Remember what you have searched on your cell while you were on duty for the past week, No? Don't worry, very soon I will hack into the Health Centre's Li-Fi and get your browsing history for the entire institute to know what you do on duty. Not only that, I won't stop until your social media accounts are hacked, and all sort of religiously and politically incorrect statements are posted. But why stop even there? Why not send manipulated photos of you with another lady or even better, another lad to your family, friends and other contacts which I will soon find out because you were stupid enough to use the Health Centre's Li-fi. And trust me there will be someone on the other end of the call when your wife or girlfriend or whoever contacts to confirm your alleged affair. And if you don't trust me, Ask anyone 'who was responsible for the infamous Turing A.I?' and they will tell you it was me." Venkatesh took out his ID-card to show Mr Pandey. "Dr Vankateshwara Iyer."

"Give me one-moment sir. I will see what I can do." the poor Mr Pandey stuttered as he ran out of his cabin sweating profusely in spite of standing directly below a ceiling fan.

"Wow, Doc! That was scary; You almost blackmailed him." Shen looked alarmed. "How did you know he was using the public Li-Fi for, let's say his 'private' business?"

"Lucky guess" Venkatesh replied with a sly smile.

"Here sir" Pandey came running in with a foldable wheelchair. "This is the newest model I could find."

"Thank you, Mr Pandey; It was a pleasure to know you." Shen acknowledged with courtesy as he took the Wheelchair from him. " Do we need to sign somewhere?"

"Just give me your name and employee number, and it would be enough sir." Mr Pandey assured. "Also if you may please return the wheelchair within a week."

"That's reasonable, I guess. So shall we proceed Dr Venkateshwara Iyer." Shen emphasised Venkatesh's full name.

"After you." Venkatesh gestured politely to Shen as they began to walk out.

"Sir! The hacking thing.." Mr Pandey stuttered nervously.

"Be a helpful man, Mr P. Pandey, like you have been today and I will make sure you succeed in remaining useful to us," Venkatesh assured with a threatening grin.

"That was dark, even for you Doc!" Shen remarked.

"I know, wasn't it." They both giggled as they got into the cab waiting for them outside the health centre.

#

"What took you guys so long to borrow a wheelchair." Anna demanded, when they arrived.

"Threatening a guy until he almost wet his pants," Venkatesh answered with a smug smile.

Chapter 13

"But Doc! I was wondering can you not reprogram Isaac not to be afraid of walking? Shen suggested as he walked in with the wheelchair.

"It won't be feasible. Isaac's fear is his self-programming, it must be he who reprograms himself not to be afraid." Venkatesh explained. "If I interfere with his programming every time he does something that we don't like then he will never be able to develop self-consciousness and always be an intelligent slave droid."

"And what about hypnotism?" Shen inquired "That is essentially reprogramming the human brain which is used to cure phobias, isn't it?"

"One can't blame you to think of hypnotism as a magical solution to phobias." Anna giggled. "But in reality, hypnotism put the person in a more susceptible state; even then one can't be forced to do anything that one considers morally wrong or doesn't want to do. Besides Isaac can't even understand language. How do you think we will cure him, even if we were somehow able to hypnotise him?"

"I can increase his trust coefficient for you to increase his susceptibility," Venkatesh mentioned while unfolding the wheelchair in front of Isaac.

"No! no more reprogramming or interfering with Isaac's

mind, there are other ways to cure phobias, and we are going to try them." Anna commanded.

"How?" Both Shen and Venkatesh asked in chorus.

"And I thought you would never ask," Anna replied with a grin. "Venkatesh, I want you to compile a video of people falling down and then getting up and walking back, can be on anything, Ice, oil, slippery floor doesn't matter as long as they can stand back upright without much injury."

"And how would that help?" Venkatesh inquired?

"Isaac will see them in his dreams; if you have programmed him like a human baby, he will have no recollection of them when he wakes up and yet they will be stored in his memory. The next time he falls, it will trigger his memory to minimise the damage from fall as done by the people in those videos. If you can find a V.R video, even better." Anna turned towards Shen. "As for you Shen, I want you to design a walker for Isaac with extendable legs so that we can slowly expose him to carry his weight on his legs with the assurance that he won't fall even if he slips."

"That will take time" Shen replied. "But consider it done."

"And Venkatesh? What about you" Anna inquired.

"Already writing a programme that will search the internet for specific videos and stream them directly into Isaac's brain," Venkatesh informed, furiously typing into his tablet.

"No shortcuts Venkatesh! I want you to check these videos manually for their content and add Mozart's Symphony in the background." Anna instructed.

"But that will take time," Venkatesh complained.

"It is ok, you have got the whole night and dreams only lasts for 5 to 10 minutes." Anna consoled.

"And what will you do while we work?" Shen asked Anna.

"Take Isaac home and see what he likes to eat so that they can be used for positive reinforcement while he goes through the exposure therapy," Anna informed them.

"You want to take Isaac home and cook for him, don't you?" Venkatesh realised.

"Ah! You cracked the mystery Doc!" Shen retorted.

"Yes! but before the two of you get busy, I need you two to carry Isaac up from his chair into this Wheelchair" Anna pointed at the wheelchair.

"Isaac is not going to like it much" Venkatesh warned.

"He won't like the rest that I have planned for him either," Anna answered with a sigh. "Hurry up! Get going you two; I will order the cab."

Venkatesh and Shen went and stood right beside Isaac's chair. Anna stood behind his chair holding the wheelchair. Shen put his arm under Isaac's right arm and held onto it with his left. Venkatesh did the same with Isaac's left arm. Isaac was unaware of what they planned to do and kept looking at both with curiosity.

"Ok, we do it when I say Anna's name out loud! OK?" Venkatesh informed. "Lift using your legs Shen. Anna! You ready?" Anna affirmed. Venkatesh looked at Isaac, "Ok, Isaac!" Venkatesh took a deep breath as Isaac looked at him. Venkatesh suddenly looked up at the ceiling. "Anna!" he gave the signal and Isaac looked up. Venkatesh and Shen quickly lifted him up in one swoop while Anna grabbed his chair and pulled it sideways and replaced it with the wheelchair as Shen and Venkatesh lowered Isaac on it. Even before Isaac could give out the first sound of a cry, he was in his new chair. Anna rushed forward to pacify Isaac if he started to cry but he didn't. Instead, he was looking at both Shen and Venkatesh with a smile. He lifted both his hands as they had done while picking him up, giggled a bit and said "Anna."

"Aww! He liked it; He thought you both were playing with him." Anna smiled kissing Isaac on his forehead.

Isaac smiled and looked at both Shen and Venkatesh while keeping his arms up. "Anna." He said.

"I think he wants us to do that again Doc!" Shen deduced. "Should we?"

"Yes! It is important for every child to get played with." Anna coaxed them.

"Very well! Let's do it again." Venkatesh agreed. "Back to positions. Hold the wheelchair firmly Anna."

Venkatesh and Shen did the same exercise again and again until they were exhausted and Isaac grew used to the sensation of being lifted and put down.

"Shouldn't Isaac be afraid of falling?" Shen pointed out while panting.

"Yes! And all we have been doing for the past 15 minutes is simulating the falling sensation for him." Venkatesh declared with heavy breaths as he supported his weight against Isaac's wheelchair. "How come he is afraid of walking, but not scared of being lifted up and put down?"

"You are a brilliant idiot! Aren't you?" Anna retorted looking at an out of breath Venkatesh. "The cab is here, enough fooling around, get back to work you two," Anna instructed as she drove away Isaac's chair out of the lab. Isaac kept staring back at the two of them and back at Anna with a gloomy face. "Dad will come home tonight," Anna whispered in Isaac's ears.

"Brilliant idiot huh Doc! That time of the month you think?" Shen asked Venkatesh after Anna had left.

"I don't just 'think'," Venkatesh answered turning to his workstation.

"Very well! I have found and ordered a Walker online. They will deliver it first thing in the morning." Informed

Shen. "So, I am retiring for the night while you burn the midnight oil."

"Wait! Where do you think you are going leaving me alone in the lab!" Venkatesh demanded.

"Oh! I don't just 'think' Doc!" Shen jibed as he walked out of the door ignoring Venkatesh.

Chapter 14

Anna's apartment in the campus was on the ground floor as all other senior Professor had and hence it was relatively convenient for her to take Isaac into her home. After they arrived, Anna switched on the toddler's channel on her on demand network Television which successfully caught Isaac's attention as she went to change. When she came out to the living room, she was happy to see Isaac smiling looking at the screen which was showing an animated teddy bear riding on a mining rail cart in an apparently evacuated mine. "Is Isaac able to relate his condition of being in a wheelchair to that of the Bear? Is he developing empathy so quickly?" Anna wondered. "Nah! Must be the catchy music and colourful visuals." She concluded.

Anna ordered small portions of assorted flavours of ice cream online to see which flavour Isaac liked best. After that, she connected her cell to the T.V wirelessly and gave it to Isaac as she drove Isaac's chair in front of her kitchen entrance.

"What would Isaac love to eat? Mama will cook for him" Anna asked, gently pinching a Smiling Isaac's cheeks. "Fried Chicken?"

Isaac smiled as he kept staring at her.

"Not impressive enough, no problem. Anna will cook something special for Isaac." Anna said lovingly. "What about meatloaf with shredded Italian cheese?"

"Anna" Isaac beamed at her.

"Aww! That sounds yummy. Doesn't it?"

"Anna" Isaac smiled radiantly.

" Ok Isaac, sit here and watch as mama cooks," Anna instructed her as she went on to cook, first Setting the oven to preheat and then mixing all the ingredients. She pointed out and named each ingredient to him and described all her activities as Isaac sat there keenly watching Anna prepare a delicious dinner.

After she put the loaf to bake in the oven, she came out of the kitchen along with Isaac and sat on the couch with Isaac's wheelchair beside her as both watched cartoons on the T.V. Sometime later the doorbell rang.

"Oh! It looks like dad's here." Anna imitated Venkatesh's deep voice as Isaac Chuckled. Then she opened the door to find the hovering drone in front of her face with a pixilated grin on its LED screen and an ice-cold package in its cargo container.

"Yay! The ice-cream is here." Anna announced as she clapped her hands looking at Isaac. Isaac smiled back.

She took the Ice-cream package from the drone and paid her dues, and the drone flew away. Then Anna placed the carton on the dining table as she opened it to reveal six cups of assorted flavours of ice cream including the classics like vanilla and chocolate.

"Will Isaac have ice cream?" Anna asked Isaac while nodding her head slowly. "Will Isaac have ice-cream?" she repeated. Isaac noticed the movement of Anna's face. "Anna" Isaac nodded in reply.

"Oh! Isaac will have ice-cream with Anna." She announced as she carried the carton with the six cups in it. She took the vanilla ice cream out of the pack and placed the rest on the coffee table. She took a spoonful of it and held it in front of Isaac. Isaac looked curiously at the cold and white emulsion. Anna realised that Isaac had never eaten anything and probably didn't know how to, so she demonstrated by eating the first spoonful of ice cream herself. Then she took another scoop and held it in front of Isaac's mouth as she opened her mouth to demonstrate. Isaac followed her and opened his mouth. Anna was surprised to see how dry it was but as soon as she placed the ice-cream on his silicone tongue, the artificial saliva glands detected it and Isaac's mouth was visibly moist within seconds. Anna gently closed Isaac's mouth by pushing up his lower jaw, and he swallowed the portion thanks to his programmed reflexes. Isaac's spectral analyser detected the fat, sugar and other organic components in the ice-cream and Isaac beamed a smile of apparent ecstasy toward Anna.

"Isaac loved the ice cream?" Anna inquired taking another scoop from the cup.

"I-Kim" Isaac repeated nodding his head. And Anna jumped up with joy. Her qualification and years of research experience had made her mind keen enough to realise what Isaac just did. Isaac was not just repeating words but communicating. He was using a combination of verbal and non-verbal means to express a thought, which was that he liked Ice-cream. Not just that but Isaac was able to figure out when a question has been asked based upon the way the words are uttered and answer it back. Isaac was finally speaking. Anna quickly dialled Venkatesh's number on her cell and waited for him to pick up. She wanted to give the news of Isaac's progress to him immediately, but then she suddenly disconnected the call.

"We won't tell Venkatesh how smart Isaac is. We will show him. What say you?" Anna asked looking at Isaac. Isaac replied with a smile as he repeated her name. Anna went back to feeding him different flavours of ice cream to see which one he liked best; she took the name of each flavour as she put them in his mouth. 'Kiwi' turned out to be his favourite. Anna was teaching Isaac how to pronounce 'Kiwi' correctly when her phone rang. Venkatesh was calling her.

She was contemplating what excuse to give Venkatesh for calling him when suddenly the oven chimed to notify that the meatloaf was ready. Anna got the reason she was looking for, without any further delay she handed Isaac the ice-cream cup and spoon and picked up the call.

"Hello! Venkatesh here, you called?" Venkatesh inquired from the other end.

"Yes! Thought you were busy so disconnected the call" Anna replied. "I have cooked meat…" Anna froze mid-sentence. It struck her suddenly that Venkatesh was vegetarian. "Stupid Anna" she scolded herself.

"What? What did you say? I think the signal is disturbed here." Venkatesh theorised.

"I said that I have cooked Meatloaf, but since you are vegetarian, you are not going to eat that even if you have to sleep on an empty stomach." She rebuked him. "So, the question is what you would like me to cook for you and is it ok if I feed meat to Isaac?" She had barely completed her sentence when she heard a sharp wail. She turned back to see Isaac had dropped the ice-cream spoon on his lap and was holding his head with one hand and the ice cream cup with another which was almost empty save a few scoops. She quickly went to him and took the ice-cream cup out of his hand and put it on the coffee table and pushed it out of his reach. Then she put the phone back to her ear.

"Why did you built Isaac to have a brain freeze?" Asked Anna annoyingly.

"What? What was that crying I heard? Is Isaac all right?" Venkatesh requested in a panic.

"Relax! He is perfectly fine. I had order ice cream for him, and he took a liking to them. Unfortunately for him he was eating it too quickly and experienced a brain freeze. Why did you build him like that?"

"So that he could experience the world like a normal human being. Wasn't that the whole point of making a machine as identical as possible to a human baby so that it can grow up to be a near perfect human?"

"With such minute details?" Anna asked staring at Isaac, holding and stroking his hair.

"Don't blame me for being thorough. I have limitations for I am only a genius after all." Venkatesh retorted.

"Forget it! No use arguing with you. When are you coming and what do I cook for you?" Anna inquired.

"I will take a couple of hours more, manually checking them takes time, but god they are funny. Leave a couple of sandwiches for me in the fridge and don't forget to add me to the guest list for your security system. I don't want to go to jail for breaking an entry in your house."

"Very well I will and don't worry you already are on the list." Anna's cheeks blushed, and eyebrows rose up in embarrassment "as is Shen." Anna added.

"Very well, good night then." Venkatesh disconnected the call before Anna could say anything and went back to work. Anna turned back towards Isaac to receive a pleasant Shock. Isaac was on his feet again. Not exactly standing upright for his back was arched forward and right arm extended ahead as he was trying to grab the Styrofoam cup. Isaac was holding onto his wheelchair's armrest firmly with his left hand and even though his knees were bent and Isaac wasn't upright. He was supporting his weight on his feet so that he could get hold of that ice cream.

"Ah! So, ice cream did the trick. Good job Anna." She congratulated herself as Isaac caught hold of the cup and fell back in his seat.

Chapter 15

That night Venkatesh reached Anna's apartment to discover that the lights were off. He naturally assumed that Anna was asleep and Isaac in sleep mode while he was recharging. The security system recognised Venkatesh's biometric signature and gently unlocked the door to let him in, the smart lights just lit up enough so that Venkatesh could make his way around the room without bumping into pieces of furniture and yet they were not bright enough to hurt his eyes which had adjusted to the dark.

He opened the fridge to find a few sandwiches and a can of baked beans on the front shelf and a carton of juice on the side racks. Venkatesh took them all out as he closed the door with a sway of his hips. Emptied the contents of the can into a plastic bowl and placed the beans and sandwiched in the microwave oven to thaw as he took a drink of cold cranberry juice. Then he proceeded to the private bedroom where Anna was sleeping on the bed, and Isaac was in his wheelchair beside Anna, connected to the power outlet. He unplugged Isaac's charger. Drove his chair to the other side of the bed and positioned it facing toward Anna as he slowly picked up Isaac's legs and put them on the bed, followed by picking up and placing his upper body besides Anna. Then he connected the charger back to the power outlet and covered Isaac with a blanket as he put a pillow under his head. Then Venkatesh took out his tablet and sat beside Isaac on the bed looking at his placid face under the dim light which had followed him from the living room to the bedroom. Venkatesh stroked Isaac's hair lightly as he began to upload the compiled video.

"Sweet dreams Isaac," Venkatesh whispered as he got up and left to eat his meal. While he was eating his dinner, the lights went on again in Anna's bedroom. Anna came outside rubbing her eyes to find Venkatesh eating his dinner on the dining table.

"Oh sorry! Did I wake you up? Didn't want to" Venkatesh apologised taking a bite of his sandwich.

"It's ok; I woke up to go to the bathroom. What time is it?" Anna asked groggily.

"Half past twelve. Why?" Venkatesh replied after checking his watch.

"Took you long enough. Come inside when you are done." Anna instructed.

"It's ok; I will be on the couch, you and Isaac rest on the bed," Venkatesh assured. Anna turned back to look towards her bedroom. Then she turned back at Venkatesh who was scooping up the last of the baked beans from the bowl.

"You put him to bed! that's cute for a robot like you." Anna jibed lovingly. Venkatesh blushed with his mouth full of baked beans which he swallowed quickly and cleaned his mouth with the back of his hands.

"even though he is in sleep mode his brain is still processing the data collected throughout the day," Venkatesh explained. "and like any human, he sleeps well when he is lying on a soft bed covered with sheets to keep him warm."

"Doesn't make it any less touching," Anna remarked affectionately. "So fresh up after you are done and rest on the couch if you are adamant enough."

"No problem. See you in the morning." Venkatesh wished good night as Anna went into the bathroom first and then back into her room. Venkatesh freshened up a little and went to sleep on the sofa.

The next morning Venkatesh woke up to the refreshing aroma of hot coffee. Anna was standing over his head looking at him while holding a cup.

"Good morning Venkatesh. Here is your coffee." She placed the coffee on the coffee table. "How did you sleep last night?"

"Comfortably," Venkatesh replied with a yawn. "I wish I could share the same positivity about waking up."

"Drink the coffee and freshen up sleepy head. A lot to do today." Anna reminded while taking a bite of her omelette. "Would you mind waking up Isaac too while you are at it?"

Venkatesh went to the bathroom to freshen up. After that, he went on to wake up Isaac. The adapter of his charger showed that he had a full charge last night. Isaac woke up groggily. Beamed a radiant smile to see Venkatesh.

"Wake up Isaac. Big day today." Venkatesh reminded enthusiastically. Isaac lifted his arms up as he had last night while playing with Shen and Venkatesh. Venkatesh held on to them as he pulled him up. Then slowly lifted his torso to the wheelchair and Isaac pulled his legs back himself.

"Good boy Isaac," Venkatesh said with affection as he drove Isaac into the living room and went for his breakfast.

"Hey, Venkatesh! If Isaac can eat, doesn't he need to use the loo as well?" Anna asked, and Venkatesh spat out the milk he was drinking because of his laughter. Imagining Isaac sitting on the porcelain throne was hilarious to him. "Of course not. Why would Shen build him with such intricacies?" Venkatesh asked, wiping the spilt milk with a napkin. "He has a compartment in his abdomen where the food is stored for anaerobic reduction. After that, we can take out the box, empty it and put it back. Although it does require cleaning and a fresh culture of electrogenic bacteria from time to time."

"Wow! You guys are through!" Anna admired astoundingly. "I didn't think Shen will put bacteria in Isaac to digest the food, but why?"

"Why! These bacteria are a part of a biological fuel cell." Venkatesh explained. "They break down the food that Isaac eats to produce carbon dioxide, which he breaths out, and electricity. Although it won't be able to drive his muscles, they are enough to keep his circuits operative in a standby mode."

"Wow! Isaac is almost human." Anna admired with awe.

"couldn't help it. Shen had to contact the Biochemical department for this piece of equipment particularly. After all both Shen and I were indoctrinated from our childhood not to waste food."

"Exactly! So, think about what you just did by spilling the milk and finish your breakfast quickly. We have a long day ahead." Anna reminded Venkatesh as he increased his pace of eating. After they were ready, they ordered a cab and called Shen.

"Yes! I am just entering the lab; they messaged me to inform that they are on their way to deliver the Walker. Where are you guys?" Shen inquired as he unlocked the lab.

"We are on our way, I have just ordered the cab, we shall leave as soon as it arrives, till then do me a favour and order a tub of kiwi ice-cream," Anna instructed.

"Ice-cream? What's the occasion, Anna?" Shen inquired suspiciously. "Don't tell me you and Venkatesh did it last night! Did you?"

"Shut up Shen! Nothing like that." Anna blushed. "The occasion is that Isaac will get on his feet today. Now hurry up. The cab is here already."

"Consider it done. Come quickly." Shen hung up.

#

By the time Venkatesh, Anna and Isaac had reached the

lab the parcel carrying the walker had already arrived, and Shen was busy opening it.

"They just delivered the Walker. The ice cream is on its way." Shen informed.

"Very well now before we begin I need to tell you that last night Isaac was successfully standing with bent knees to reach a cup of ice cream," Anna informed. "No points for guessing the flavour."

"Wow! Increasing his affinity for fat was a good idea after all." Contemplated Venkatesh.

"Not yours." Shen corrected. "It was Anna's idea."

"We work as a team Shen," Venkatesh remarked.

"Finally, you admit Doc! That calls for doubling the order for ice cream." Shen retorted.

"And as I was saying before you two so rudely interrupted. Isaac is learning to communicate."

"What, How, When?" Shen demanded in amazement.

"What were you two up to last night?" Venkatesh asked with awe.

"Not much! But my theory is he can differentiate between a question and a statement by the difference in the tone of the voice." Anna informed. "But for now, concentrate on getting him to walk."

"How?" Shen asked.

"Like we have taught him to do other stuff. By showing him how to use a walker to walk."

"And I guess ice cream will provide the required motivation." Venkatesh reasoned.

"You indeed are a genius Doc! Oh! The ice cream is here," Shen informed as he felt his cell vibrate and rushed outside to get the delivery.

"Go on Venkatesh. Show him how to use the walker." Anna coaxed Venkatesh to demonstrate the use of Walker to Isaac which he did. As Isaac was built almost the same height as Venkatesh, the walker didn't require separate height adjustments. After Venkatesh had demonstrated how to use the walker, Anna placed the walker in front of Isaac and Shen was instructed to stand a few steps away with the open tub of ice-cream. As soon as Isaac's olfactory sensors detected the kiwi flavour his eyes sparkled.

"Kiwi I-Kim," Isaac said as he longingly extended his arms toward Shen. Shen didn't move. Isaac looked at Anna who was pretending to read a book.

"Anna kiwi I-Kim." He pleaded looking at her which she pretended to ignore. Venkatesh could hardly stop himself from jumping up with excitement as he realised that Isaac was trying to get Anna's attention toward the ice-cream. Anna was right, Isaac was communicating verbally. When Isaac understood that none would help him, he extended his legs from the footrest of the wheelchair onto the floor and began to drag his wheelchair with his strides. He was using his legs to move while he was still sitting. Anna did not anticipate this brilliant move from Isaac, However, without giving a second thought, she took a scoop of ice cream from the tub, feed it to Isaac while he was cheerfully looking at her.

"Wasn't he supposed to..." Venkatesh was silenced off by Anna before he could finish. Anna signalled him to pretend to be busy while she handed the spoon to Isaac and started to reread the book.

Isaac tried to get Anna's attention again, but she didn't budge. He tried to drag his wheelchair again, but this time it didn't move either. It was then that Venkatesh noticed that the handbrake on the side of the chair was engaged. Anna had stealthily pulled the lever when she fed Isaac, and poor Isaac had no idea of this trickery. Finally, having realised that he had no other option than to brave a fall, Isaac looked once more around the lab and then on the floor and let out a deep breath. Slowly he pulled himself up to his feet by grabbing onto the handles of the walker and cautiously took a step forward. When Isaac realised that he didn't need to balance his weight if he had the walker he felt a little secure and moved towards Shen. After Isaac had eaten a few scoops, Shen was instructed by Anna to get further away from Isaac, which he did. Isaac again reached him leaning on the walker. Finally, when Anna was confident enough that Isaac won't fall again, she walked to Isaac and tried to pull the walker away from him. Isaac resisted. He tightened his grip to the point that it would have almost dented the handles.

Anna held Isaac's face in her hands and looked deeply into his eyes. She gently removed her right hand and placed it on Isaac's clenched fist. Anna slowly shifted her gaze to Isaac's feet as Isaac followed.

"Trust me! You won't fall." Anna whispered.

"Anna," Isaac whispered back as he looked back into her eyes, slowly loosening his grip. Anna gently took the Walker away, Supporting his body on her own, she slowly moved closer now that the walker was no longer between them and hugged him, gently pushing him upright. As she slowly walked back, Venkatesh and Shen saw with their jaws dropped. Isaac was standing upright without any support. As they watched in amazement, Isaac slowly began to walk forward. Cautiously he made his way toward Shen, slowly but surely, he was getting close to the ice cream tub as the whole gang watched each of his steps in utter disbelief for he had never walked with such determination. When finally, he reached Shen, he took the Ice cream container from Shen who was looking at Isaac with his mouth open.

"Shen, I-Kim?" Isaac asked. Isaac did not merely utter the words, but he asked. Shen couldn't hold a teardrop from slipping down his eyes as he hugged Isaac over the tub. Venkatesh rushed towards Anna and hugged her tightly.

"Thank you! Thank you so much, Anna." He whispered in her ears. He looked at her face, and they were wet with tears. Venkatesh began to wipe them off affectionately as Anna closed her eyes and swiftly pressed her lips against those of

Venkatesh. His mind went blank. Time seemed to pause all around him, and all sounds damped down. His body began to relax as his mind calmed, and in this moment of tranquillity Venkatesh kissed her. Slowly, gently, delicately, treating her with utmost care like a precious gem that she was.

Their peace was suddenly disturbed by a cry. Anna broke their embrace and turned to see Shen sitting in Isaac's wheelchair which was turned towards them. Shen was holding his head with one hand and bumping it with the open palm of the other with the ice-cream spoon on the floor near his feet, and the tub on his lap and Isaac was standing beside him, looking down towards him with curiosity.

"Just a meagre brain freeze." Anna diagnosed. "want to continue?" She looked at Venkatesh encircling her arms around his neck.

"with pleasure." Venkatesh went back to kissing her.

Chapter 16

Soon, Venkatesh moved in with Anna along with Isaac. Shen returned his apartment keys to the institute and moved into Venkatesh's now empty apartment. The rule of their institute dictated that Shen couldn't be given a similar sized apartment as that of Venkatesh and Anna because of his lack of the required qualification. So Venkatesh never informed the authorities of their apartment's switch.

#

Isaac, being an advanced A.I was a quick study. By the end of a year, he had completed the high school level education. Was proficient in the use of language and mastered his motor skills. Then one day, Anna suggested that Isaac should be sent to school to have his first interaction with people other than the three of them.Venkatesh vehemently disagreed arguing that immature teenagers with their surging hormones and confused emotions would be too much for Isaac, and he will only end up being confused, besides he had nothing new to learn there either, especially not at their pace. In the end, however, Venkatesh had to talk to the school principal to let Isaac attend high school. She agreed on the condition that no one can come to know that Isaac is an android created by Venkatesh and that Isaac must wear the school uniform.

Venkatesh agreed to this and the next day he came to drop Isaac off at the school in full school uniform which included full sleeves white shirt with maroon tie and grey trousers. They covered the entire body of Isaac but his hands and above the neck and rendered him indistinguishable from any other human student by appearance. Isaac was initially reluctant to venture forth in this new environment all alone, but Venkatesh comforted him by assuring that Schools are made to be a safe environment for children and since he was much superior to any of them in physical resilience and intellect, hee had nothing to worry. Also, he would get to observe and interact with another human as well. With the exciting and encouraging words from Venkatesh, Isaac set forth on his new adventures.

Unfortunately, hardly a few hours had gone by when Venkatesh was called by Isaac's school principal to meet her. When Venkatesh and Anna reached the principal's office, they found a middle-aged pot-bellied man with a checked shirt and bushy moustache sitting across the principal's desk with an anguished look. The principal informed them that Isaac had started a rebellion in the 12th grade. Curious, when they asked for further details, the principal told them that in Isaac's class, the faculty punished someone corporally. Before the teacher could use his cane again, Isaac stopped him. When the teacher commanded to let go of his hand, Isaac complied; only to stop him again as he attempted to cane the student. Isaac brazenly told the faculty that he would not let his friend come to any harm.

"And when I raised my cane to punish him for his misbehaviour, He snatched the cane and broke it into four pieces, saying he cannot let me harm him either." The moustached man complained. "He even refused to apologise saying he has done no wrong and asked me to prove if he had. When I said a student ought to obey his teacher, he said something about the absence of such commands in 'his programming' Now the whole class is cheering him and won't let me take my lecture!"

Venkatesh burst out laughing on hearing the news, as Anna shot the pot-bellied faculty with a look of anguish. "I told you school wouldn't do any good." Venkatesh poked Anna with his elbow. "I stand corrected, I never knew it would be this fun the first day itself." Venkatesh looked at the principal who was staring at him in disbelief. "Did he address his fellow student as 'friend'? Anyway, where is Isaac? I guess he has learned all that you could teach him. It's time to take him back."

When Venkatesh and Anna reached Isaac's classroom, it was already lunchtime. The class was empty, save for Isaac and a cute, blonde haired, white skinned and hazel eyed girl who was sharing her lunch with him. She said her name was Samantha and she didn't want Isaac to stay hungry for the rest of the day as he had been punished not to go to the cafeteria. Anna lovingly brushed her silky locks as she told her the secret of Isaac. Venkatesh had to make Isaac unbutton his shirt to show her the artificial skin underneath. Samantha observed with widened eyes and, holding a morsel in front of her open mouth, but too distracted to eat it. Venkatesh promised her that she could come to visit Isaac if she never told anyone about him in the School. Venkatesh also encouraged her to continue their protest and tell everyone that Isaac was going to another school to save their students. Anna kept staring at him, with eyes wide with disbelief.

While they were returning from the school, Isaac was curious at people's inclination toward violence.

"You see Isaac; people love violence. They love it in a similar way you love Kiwi ice cream." Anna informed. "During evolution, aggressive behaviour has helped vertebrates to acquire and protect food, territory, mate and offspring and hence it has become as rewarding a factor as food."

"But the laws suggest strict punishment for such behaviours, which can't be beneficial for survival in the present scenario," Isaac argued.

"And hence we need to continue our evolution, to evolve into a more civilised people than our ancestors were," Venkatesh remarked as the cab took them home.

#

After the school fiasco, the team decided to homeschool Isaac. But they soon found out that what took the three of them decades, Isaac could learn all of it in months. Running out of subjects to teach, they contacted the other departments of their institute and their respective heads to let Isaac study in their class. The students in other departments were much tolerant towards Isaac and treated him well. Isaac seemed to love the interactions he had with his peers until about six months passed.

The management received the news that Isaac was so brilliant that the faculties were using him to take their lectures while they would focus on their projects or casually pass their free time. The students, however, loved how Isaac could solve all their problems and patiently taught them, without ever scolding or punishing them for not completing their assignments or coming late to the lecture. He was, as his classmates described 'The coolest' professor ever. The management took a personal offence at the ease with which their employees and students were living their life and forbade Isaac ever to attend any lectures in any department ever again. The order infuriated Venkatesh at first, but when he discovered that Isaac had already gained masters level knowledge in the different fields taught in other departments, he obliged.

Chapter 17

After about two and a half years of Isaac's activation, Anna became pregnant with Venkatesh's child. Very soon, Anna understood the frustration of the Institute's management with Isaac, when she realised that Venkatesh was using Isaac the same way as those other faculties had, to escape from their responsibilities. Venkatesh and Shen would collect all the books and files they could find on child care and give it to Isaac who was within weeks, more capable of taking care of Anna than both the men ever hoped or worked for. So, while Anna was on her maternal leave, being taken care by Isaac, which she adored. Venkatesh and Shen were having fun together while working on other projects. Unfortunately, whenever Anna would get mad on any one of them, they would remind her that Isaac was the most knowledgeable nurse she could have, which was entirely right, but it didn't make Anna complain any less about Venkatesh running away from his responsibilities.

So, after three years and a few, single child custody threats from Anna, Venkatesh found himself in the maternity ward of the hospital, holding Anna's hand as she was writhing in labour and cursing and accusing Venkatesh of her misery. Shen and Isaac were impatiently waiting outside for the last one hour when the cries of Anna reached such a peak that her agony was palpable even to those waiting outside the ward. Isaac was inching closer to cracking the tiled floor with his nervous foot taps when Shen suggested meditation. Seating with a forward hunch and with his arms stretched and held onto the edges of the bench tightly beside both his thighs, Isaac was too uncertain to not focus on Anna.

"Why do people celebrate the birth of a child when it causes so much pain?" Isaac asked an unprepared Shen.

"It is all because of biology," Shen said after giving a thought. "It designs the babies to be irresistibly cute, the younger they are, the cuter they get, Plus the mother's biology conspires to bribe her mind with oxytocin, it makes them go even mushier. I guess something equally messed up happens with the guys too."

"It must be hard, for Dr Venkateshwara to see her in pain." Isaac acknowledged staring at the wooden doors of the maternity ward as Anna screamed again. "Particularly when he knows that he plays a major part in her pain and yet share none of it."

"Oh! Trust me; Anna will make sure he suffers." Shen assured with a grin.

About an hour later the nurse came out to call Isaac and Shen in. When they reached inside, Anna was lying on the delivery table in her hospital gown, drenched in sweat but smiling. Visibly exhausted but understandably ecstatic. Venkatesh was laughing with tears rolling down his eyes as he adoringly stared at his baby. Shen hugged Anna and wiped the sweat from her face. Venkatesh handed over the child to Isaac. Addressing him as Isaac's little brother. Isaac cautiously took his little brother in his arms and gently rocked him as Isaac stared into his deep dark eyes. The child opened his lips and gave a small smile before beginning to cry out loud. The nurse politely instructed all but the newborn and the mother to get out of the delivery room and handed back the baby to Anna to feed him.

#

Anna's baby was named Samath; it translated to 'King' in Telugu. Venkatesh's native language, faithful to Venkatesh's words, Isaac proved to be the best nurse Samath could get. Even though he could take care of the baby all by himself; apart from feeding, but he insisted that Anna be the one to nurse him since it was essential in the primary years for the baby to bond with his mother. Only in the night when both Venkatesh and Anna would be asleep, did Isaac took the sole responsibility of Samath, sleeping and charging in the baby's room so that Anna and Venkatesh could sleep undisturbed. Since Venkatesh had programmed Isaac to stay in sleep mode while charging and requiring minimum eight hours of 'sleep' per day, Isaac had to reprogram himself so that he could take small and light naps scattered throughout the day to complete his quota. Isaac even recalibrated his auditory and olfactory sensors to be vigilant throughout his sleep so that he would wake up when Samath required attention.

#

After almost a year of the birth of Samath, On Isaac's 4th birthday, i.e. after four years of his activation, Anna sat down with him to explain to him about the effect of anonymity on human behaviour. She recounted the legend of the ring of Gyges and H.G well's 'The invisible man' to exemplify the degradation of moral character and boldness of expression that anonymity can provide in the real world, with the help of the Internet. Venkatesh deleted the line of codes that stopped Isaac from accessing the net but instructed him to use it only to observe and learn about human behaviour and warned him to be cautious of any hacking attempts. Now; The whole world was accessible to Isaac to learn from. He started learning about different people, their cultures their traditions and their opinions in real time about current events happening around the world, with no end of the syllabus and no restrictions from any management.

In the following few months, Anna observed a drastic reduction in Isaac's queries about humanity. Initially, she assumed it was because of his access to the internet, but later the Li-Fi bill showed that after an initial surge in the band usage for a few weeks after Isaac's birthday, the data consumption had drastically reduced. Isaac wasn't using the net to educate himself about humans anymore. When she confronted him one day to ask about it, he informed them that he had identified and understood human, even though their large population. Each of them wasn't as unique as others thought. Each human Isaac concluded was a collection of a combination of identifiable characteristic. The combination of those in addition to one's circumstances and social, political and economic status gave them an individualistic identity and expression for sure, yet Isaac had not come across any different characteristic or emotion that he hadn't encountered before in his first few weeks of access to the internet.

When Anna informed Venkatesh about this, the news left him pleasantly surprised. He expected a day like this would come as Isaac was programmed to analyse and understand human. She argued that people are not that generic and can't be 'solved' so quickly. Venkatesh assured that Isaac was much more capable than a human and he had the advantage of the thorough knowledge of the history of humanity and psychology. One day, Isaac was bound to find some common repetitive patterns in every human he interacted with. And to prove Isaac understanding of Human and the human consciousness, Venkatesh decided it was high time to present and test Isaac on an International scientific conference.

Chapter 18

Soon enough, Venkatesh presented Isaac at the International Conference on Artificial Intelligence and Application (AIAPP) in Geneva Switzerland. Various experts tested Isaac in different versions of the Turing test, Imitation game and Cons Scale test and even though Isaac failed in some of them, most of the experts agreed that his performance was no less than astonishing. Soon the international media was covering Isaac's story and titled him Actual Intelligence (A.I).

Back home, Venkatesh and his team received a request from Susan Philip for another exclusive. Reluctant at first, he later agreed after some persuasion from Anna. Shen decided it was better to avoid Susan and excused himself from the interview on the pretext of babysitting Samath. Unlike the previous time, Anna's apartment was chosen as the location for the meeting, and Shen stayed in Venkatesh's apartment with baby Samath. After her crew had set up their equipment and Venkatesh, Anna and Isaac were seated on Anna's couch in her living room, with Susan on a single seater adjacent to them, the interview started. After a brief introduction of the three of them, Susan turned toward Venkatesh with her questions.

"So, Dr Venkateshwara and Dr Anna, first, congratulations on the birth of your first child and the international success and fame for your brainchild, Isaac the robot." Susan congratulated the three of them with a smile and handshakes.

"Thank you, Ms Susan, we would also like to extend the congratulations to you for the launch of your new on-demand network." Anna congratulated her back.

"And many thanks for agreeing to this interview." Susan bowed her head slightly placing her palm on her chest. "I guess this is our third interview about Isaac, Isn't it Dr Venkatesh?"

"Second actually, the first was about the Turing A.I." Venkatesh pointed out adjusting his tie's knot.

"Yes! Exactly." Susan recalled, casting a quick glance at the ceiling and back. "And that reminds me that Isaac qualified many of the Turing tests conducted in Geneva. Care to explain what they are and what does it mean."

"Well, Turing test is an experiment where a person interacts with an A.I and another person and tries to identify which one is which, based solely on their communication, nothing else," Venkatesh emphasised with a quick swipe of his hand in the air. "And qualifying the tests means that a robot is indistinguishable from a human to the examiner."

"And I guess the Turing A.I did it as well? So, what's the difference?" Susan narrowed her eyes.

"Oh! The differences are huge!" Anna exclaimed with raised eyebrows. "First of all, the judges were experts; there were many variations of the test that Isaac had to pass, one of them was the reverse Turing test, where Isaac had to identify a man from a machine exclusively based on their text-based communication. Then there was the empathy test, where Isaac was shown different videos of the various people under different circumstances and asked to guess what those people were likely feeling, and he scored satisfactorily in each of them.

"So, does that mean that Isaac has a consciousness." Susan leaned forward with intrigue.

"Susan, the problem with consciousness is that it is hard to define and almost impossible to prove its presence, for example, all the test of consciousness is based on the subject's response, and we have no way to know what is going on in the subject's mind," Anna explained.

"So basically, Dr Anna, what you are trying to say is, even you don't know whether Isaac has consciousness or not and the tests haven't clarified it in any way. Right?" Susan passed a sly smile towards her.

"Ms Susan! can you be sure that that Dr Venkatesh, Dr Anna or any of your crew member have consciousness?" Isaac asked staring towards the cameraman.

"I don't get what you mean Isaac, of course, we are all conscious, what's there to prove?" Susan asked with a puzzled look on her face.

"Ms Susan, have you played virtual reality games?"

"Yes, I have, when I was young," Susan crossed her legs as she replied.

"Now consider the non-playable characters in the game that you interacted with, for instance, the boss at the end of a level, the villager who sent you on a quest, the general of your army who gave you war reports. If given adequate processing power, these characters would appear to have a consciousness of their own, won't they?" Isaac stared at Susan with a smile.

"But we are not in a game now. This world is the real deal." Susan defended, perplexed at Isaac's argument.

"Trust me, Ms Susan, A good enough simulation will appear real to you if only you forget when and if you pushed the 'start' button, like dreams seems real while one dream and yet one has no recollection of where and when did the dream start." Isaac leaned back into the pillows as he continued. "The point is one can never know if anyone else in this world is conscious or very successful at pretending to be conscious and that doesn't even actually matter to humans as you assume others to have a consciousness like you; be it a dog, cat or the universe itself."

"Wow! I can plainly see why the scientists were so impressed." Susan shook her head in disbelief and admiration.

"Exactly!" Anna agreed and patted on Isaac's back. "Even if we talk about the sensations, emotions and experience that the human mind has to external agents. They are widely subjective and varies on a lot of issues, for instance, someone may love arts and literature, and someone else might be indifferent to it. The parameters of beauty are diverse throughout the world and according to one's culture. It's hard to establish what should one feel about anything or even if they should feel anything about a particular thing or not."

"I can't even pretend to understand the half of your arguments, but I do understand that even Isaac failed in some of the tests." Susan looked at Venkatesh. "Care to explain what they were and why did Isaac fail."

"Well yes, Isaac was caught twice as an A.I." Venkatesh nodded with reluctance while shutting his eyes tightly. "Once when he was being examined by text messages because he didn't make any spelling mistakes. The second time during an Imitation game when the examiner wasn't able to identify the sex of Isaac because he knew too well about stuff that the examiner thought any human candidate identifying with a specific gender couldn't know. The examiner concluded that only an A.I could have such deep knowledge about both the sexes."

"Ah! So, Isaac's perfection became his downfall, ironic." Susan pressed her lips together. "But I'm curious, what sex does Isaac identify itself with?"

"Both and none," Isaac replied.

"Well! That explains a lot. And now for the big question that everybody is dying to know." Susan turned towards Isaac. "Does by any chance you plan to kill us all sometime in the future?"

"Exterminate mankind?" Isaac asked in surprise. "Why? A.I do not need air to breath, a large landmass to stay, water to drink or food to eat. I have no rivalry with humanity so why would I waste resources, time and energy to kill them. Besides not only will it be an expensive endeavour but incredibly wasteful considering it is much cheaper and profitable to keep a man alive who adds value to the GDP."

"Maybe you will feel threatened someday, that humans could turn you off or disrupt your power supply," Susan argued.

"A.I contribute a significant portion of our nation's economy at a meagre operating and maintenance costs and their contribution will only increase in the future. So, a large-scale shutdown of A.I will only lead to loss and poverty which no government will like to bring upon on its economy." Isaac explained while leaning forward in his seat, tapping his thumbs together while his fingers remained interlocked. "It is not you who I feel threatened from but the enemy of our states. The problem is, I theorise that people feel threatened by A.I and they think that robots like me think along the same lines as they do."

"So, I guess there is no risk of you trying to enslave humanity either," Susan added with relief.

"Not at all! Humans are too clumsy." Isaac added with a sarcastic smile as Venkatesh and Anna started to laugh.

"Talk about some gratitude for creating you, Isaac." Anna twisted Isaac's ears playfully.

"Aren't you thankful Dr Anna that your clumsiness guarantees your freedom, which you people love the most." Isaac quipped.

"Ah! I wish most of the regular families were such a happy family like you guys." Susan signed smiling at the three of them laughing together.

"There lies the problem, Susan. They are normal." Venkatesh jibed looking at the camera as Susan bid farewell to her audience and the cameraman raised a thumb up.

Chapter 19

Anuj Johnson was considered the black sheep of the Johnson family. Unlike his other two brothers who were studious and worked hard to educate themselves so that they did not have to toil on their ancestral lands under the scorching sun and torturing humidity in their village, Anuj was a dreamer. Anuj was the youngest of the three sons and hence was never shoved with the responsibilities of earning a living. He had the luxury of dreaming and what dreams he dreamt! He dreamt of owning a business of his own, then soon he would have his chain of establishments. He will be richer than all of his brothers combined. Then he would employ his villagers in his establishment across the country and become a hero to his people, his family, and then nobody will admonish him for not getting enough marks or running away from his school with his mates to play and swim in the village pond.

However, as time passed, it became evident to him that all his troubles were due to his brothers. His parents and relatives would keep comparing them to him, their achievements against his failures and their potential against his lack of any. Whenever such arguments would break in his home, he would run out to seek comfort from the chef and owner of the line hotel on the outskirts of his village and beside the highway. The owner, Mr Krishna was his idol. He would play for hours with Krishna's son, Anil. Together they would pick on Anil's sister, little Bulbul, until she would begin to cry and Krishna would come from behind to smack them. Then Krishna would gently take Bulbul in his arms and ask the two boys to follow him into the kitchen where he would give them freshly prepared sweets and feed Bulbul with his own hands.

Krishna's restaurant was where Anuj learnt the basics of the food industry and the pleasure and satisfaction one earned by feeding people. It was customary for Krishna to visit the local temple each day after closing so that he could feed the beggars and visit the wholesale market each morning to buy the rations for the day. Krishna never kept any leftovers or vegetables in the fridge for it was his principle to serve his patrons with the freshest farm harvested ingredients.

Anuj might have been a dull student in his school, but he was the perfect apprentice to Krishna. Krishna loved him like his own children. Practically, all three of them grew up together. Like Anuj, Anil too was never too interested in studies. However, Anil had a natural knack for running a business. The two boys would often discuss how they would work at Krishna's hotel when they grew up, Anuj would cook up new dishes that nobody had ever tasted before and together they will be the richest partners in the village and later in the whole district and state as well.

Soon enough, both the boys finished their high schooling, and Anuj failed to get admission in any government-funded engineering schools, unlike his eldest brother. As usual, his own family cursed his lack of talent and hard work. He became the least favourite and the most worrisome child of his family. After the academic success of both of his brothers to get into government-funded universities, his parents cursed that he had brought shame to their household, but unfazed by the criticism; he knew, this failure was going to be the best thing his average academic life could gift him.

Mr Krishna was much more tolerant about Anil's marks. He always thought his son as his heir, the one who would take over his small establishment after he retires, all he wished was that his son was as skilful in the kitchen as Anuj. Alas! Anuj wasn't his to claim, however on Anuj's request Mr Krishna went to talk to his parents. He informed them about the educational course he had heard they teach in great Universities where one is taught to work in big hotels and restaurants, 'Hotel management'. He told them how talented and hardworking Anuj was in his kitchen and that he would flourish under proper guidance and professional training from the prominent chefs. The possibility of Anuj and Anil working together to establish a decent hotel in the nearby town so that they could live and earn here and take care of his parents, unlike his elder brothers who had gone away to live in other big cities was quite enticing to the elderly Johnsons. So, after a bit of coaxing, they finally agreed to send Anuj to a private university.

The city life was quite alien to him. The people, culture, attitude, architecture, everything was new and liberating. Initially, he found it difficult to adjust to the fast-paced city life, but soon he grew accustomed to it. He made friends, studied and partied with them. He found a home away from home, not the kind that was the Johnson household but the family that Krishna, Anil and Bulbul was to him. Unlike the stereotype through, his new-found lifestyle didn't deteriorate his determination to learn. In fact, all it did was to flame his passion, he was with people that could understand and appreciate him, and he was determined to be recognised. His first-year results came as a pleasant surprise to everyone in his village but Mr Krishna. Anuj had won the academic scholarship in his class, and his tuition fee was waived. Anuj wasn't the black ship anymore; he was the batch topper.

Anuj however, wasn't the ideal student, he wasn't the busiest or the most hardworking one either. He did get involved in some nasty fights. Wasn't very popular with his classmates, but he was passionate about cooking. He followed the instructions meticulously and then when his dishes were the textbook success, he experimented to improve upon them. These little experiments helped him to learn a lot that his other rivals didn't, and at the end of his course, he had a call letter to join as one of the line cooks in one of the best gourmet restaurant in the city. Who says jobs suck? His didn't.

He worked meticulously under the guidance of the master chefs to learn his craft, but at the end of it, automation hit the restaurant business. Hotels employing robots had existed long before he was born, this he had read in books, but they were more like a novelty than a serious business practice.

Maybe in a handful of restaurants across the globe where the super-rich or tourists went, not for the food but to brag about the experience of being served by the robots, but he had never imagined that he would experience the trend so up close and so soon.

The restaurants had brought highly sophisticated, state of the art robotic arms that could replicate every intricate movement capable by human appendages, albeit with more speed and precision than the capability of any human. The senior chefs saved their jobs because someone required to teach the robots the signature dishes of the brand and invent new ones, the line cooks weren't so lucky. Unfazed, Anuj tried to get a job in other posh restaurants, and he succeeded. After all, he had the required qualification and one-year experience, but soon enough, the machines replaced him again. The restaurant he had worked for earlier had successfully cut its cost of paying their employees by replacing them with robots, and the better quality and speed with which they prepared the food to perfection had only increased their profit. The other businesses followed suit.

Anuj realised that he wasn't going to hold a job in such eateries for long. His pride prevented him from working at any lesser establishment. So, he was stricken by the bright idea that had hit every graduate after they had completed a few years in any industry. To take the entrepreneur's way and be one's, own boss. With newfound vigour, exemplary qualification certificates, and an impressive resume and freshly cooked samples of his most delicious dishes in an insulated container, he went to the bank to ask for a loan. The receptionist courteously guided him to the newly recruited loan section officer. An A.I software.

It would be honest to admit that Anuj was perturbed initially, he even felt sorry for the poor chap who was replaced by the A.I, but he calmed himself quickly and was determined not to lose another opportunity to the machines. He presented his plans, his credentials and recommendations to the best of his abilities. He even offered the food that he had cooked which the A.I politely refused. After thoroughly analysing Anuj's data, the present trend of the hospitality industries and experts forecast it concluded that Anuj's enterprise would be viable on the currently proposed scale if he employed robots instead of humans as the cooking and serving staff.

Anuj snapped. He could have excepted a loan refusal if faced with one but the recommendation of buying workers instead of employing them was a death blow to his dream of offering jobs to the needy and be of some use to his fellow men. Had he accepted those conditions, he was sure he would have killed his soul with his bare hands, he couldn't do it. He hurriedly took back his documents as the A.I kept suggesting other alternatives to appease him. He didn't let the A.I succeed. He visited multiple banks to plead, but everywhere he found the same A.I with the same results and suggestions. Had there been any humans at the desk he might have convinced one of them, there would be hope that not every one of them will come up to the same conclusion, but now there was none. It was the same monotony throughout the city. Each restaurant Anuj visited, employed the same kind of robots from the same company, every bank had the same A.I software deciding the viability of people's dreams and hard work. The loss of his job had failed to shake him, but the loss of hope had crushed him.

Anuj returned to his village and partnered with his childhood friend Anil. They sold Mr Krishna's Hotel, took a loan from the local bank and opened a decent hotel in the nearby city. Even though this restaurant was much smaller than what Anuj dreamed of, but this was all his; and all he had. Anil didn't interfere in the matters of the kitchen. Anuj adopted his mentor's policy of using fresh ingredients and training and employing the locals. Anuj soon married Bulbul to the joy of Anil as now they were not just friends and partners but brothers as well. Albeit in-laws.

Chapter 20

One beautiful evening, when there wasn't much footfall in their hotel and Anuj was coordinating the activities of his subordinates and not actively cooking anything, all of a sudden, he heard Anil call out to him from the reception with urgency. Fearing that one of his line cooks have caused a blunder with one of the dishes and he had an angry customer complaint, he rushed out of the kitchen towards the reception. "I should have been more vigilant." He thought. "The passing years have made me lazy." When he came out of the kitchen, he saw a middle-aged man in a black cassock with the cross around his neck. 'Father Albert' was on the reception counter. However Albert wasn't looking outraged, so maybe the problem wasn't that big, but who knew, Fathers are trained to be polite. Weren't they?

"Yes, Anil! What's the trouble?" Anuj panted.

"Nothing," Anil informed as he pointed toward the single flat screen tv in the restaurant which was playing the interview of Venkatesh, Anna and Isaac with Susan Phillip along with the subtitles in the regional language. Anuj stared at it for a while reading the subtitles to get an idea of what was Anil talking about. Anil took Father Albert's order and forwarded it to the kitchen for a takeaway.

"They say this scientist has made a robot who can pass off as a human. Other scientists have verified it." Anil mentioned while counting the bills.

"Aye! Like it is ever possible for a machine to be a human." Anuj scoffed. "And what would they know, a bunch of nerds who spent their lives being buried in books, like they know what normal humans are like."

"Oh! You should listen to the answers this robot gave to the reporter's question." Anil suggested.

"Huh," Anuj snorted. "It is a mere puppet! The answers are all pre-recorded, it is only a monkey dancing to the tunes of that scientist."

"Yes! About that scientist! Doesn't he look familiar? I bet I have seen him somewhere." Anil tried to recall Venkatesh's face.

"Wait let me check, what do they say his name is?" Anuj took out his cell as he sought to read Venkatesh's name on the screen and quickly typed it and pressed enter.

"Holy God! You remember that Turing scandal? The one where a kid committed suicide under the influence of a computer programme. He created that bloody programme." Anuj broke the news. Albert who was patiently listening to the two now turned towards the screen as well, Yes indeed! Even he could recall Venkatesh's face from the scandal years ago.

"And this time he has created another robot who looks and behaves like a human, and they let him! These people call themselves smart." Anuj scoffed.

While all the three of them were staring at the T.V

screen, the waiter delivered the packaged order of Albert at the reception.

"Here is your order Father." Anil handed the parcel to Albert. "Although I would recommend that you have your dinner here while it is hot and fresh."

"Oh! This is not for me, son! My sister has returned from her college this evening. This is for her." Albert explained.

"Oh! Then you could have just called us; we would have delivered it to your home." Anuj suggested politely.

"It's ok son! I thought I should take a walk around the town while I was at it."

"As you wish Father, see you again. Goodnight." Anuj waved goodbye as he was about to walk back into the kitchen when he heard Albert call out to him. He turned back and saw Albert walking towards him with the parcel in his hands.

"Would you mind paying me a visit at the church tonight, after you have closed, that is?" Albert inquired.

"It might be a little late, about 11 I assume," Anuj replied checking the wall clock.

"I will wait, I insist that you come." Albert coaxed Anuj

"Ok Father see you later then."

"God bless you son."

#

That night after closing, Anuj borrowed Anil's bike to

visit Albert. The church was merely a couple of blocks away from their hotel, and when Anuj arrived, he found Albert waiting for him.

"You are on time son. I appreciate punctuality." Albert greeted Anuj with a radiant smile.

"Couldn't incur the sin of making a holy man wait." Anuj beamed a polite smile.

"You would have been forgiven," Albert assured.

"So, what was it that you wanted to talk about Father?" Anuj asked as he got off his bike and pocketed the key.

"I was worried about you. You looked troubled about the news of that scientist and his robot," Albert asked while putting his arm around Anuj's shoulders.

"Oh! It's fine, nothing. I was just taken back that they still let him do this after what he had done." Anuj brushed off casually.

"And you think this time he will cause bigger trouble?" Albert inquired staring into Anuj's eyes, he looked down but stayed silent. Albert began. "You don't like these intelligent machines much. do you?"

"How can I Father? Do you know how many lose their jobs every year because of them? I mean it is not exactly 'their' fault but neither does the fault lies with those who lose their daily bread because of the machines. I say that they are only human after all, they have their need to earn, limitations as well, because God created us this way, didn't he?" Anuj demanded with a sharp pain in his voice.

"Of course, and God created us that way because that was the best for us. He created angels as well, but he loves us the most." Albert comforted Anuj. "But this man. This scientist, he is trying to become a god by creating an artificial human."

"But science can't be wrong. Can it? The pursuit of knowledge is a noble thing, right?" Anuj demanded.

"Of course it is. The greatest of advancement has occurred due to science, unfortunately so have the greatest of destruction." Albert warned. "You know what happened after Adam and Eve took a bite of the forbidden fruit in the garden of Eden?"

"They were thrown out of Eden," Anuj replied. He remembered the masses he had attended during his childhood.

"Yes, as a punishment for disobeying God, but you might also remember that the apple Enlighted them, gave them the knowledge that they were naked. It shamed them." Albert narrated. "The moral of the story is that knowledge has a temptation of its own, it is powerful, it can corrupt the weak and enlighten the firm. It can bring the greatest of destruction and prove to be the biggest of a boon. For the Lord is all knowing and all loving." Albert crossed his heart as he looked up at the cross.

"So, do you mean to say this scientist, This Venkateshwara is among the weak?" Anuj demanded.

"Has he proven himself to be reliable in the past?" Albert looked sharply at Anuj.

"I guess not, I mean the last time when he was in the news it was because someone died." Anuj stared blankly towards the empty seats of the last row of the church.

"Not someone Anuj! A child, a little girl, was convinced to sin by a demonic entity that he created." Albert scorned. "The Lord was kind to forgive his ignorance last time, but do you think he learned anything?"

"You are right Father! That's what I was thinking, how come none have stopped him even when everyone knows what he did." Anuj demanded angrily.

"That I do not know son! But what I am sure of, is that someone should." Albert commanded. "Otherwise who knows how many deaths this Frankenstein's monster will be responsible for."

"I know, but I am just a cook in an ordinary hotel in a small town, what can I possibly do?" Anuj pleaded with a sigh, as he stared down at the polished floor.

"Don't underestimate yourself son." Albert held him by his shoulders. "For thou art a good man, and that is the most important thing to be." Albert slowly turned him toward the statue of Jesus. "And all it takes for evil to win, is that good men do nothing."

That night as Anuj rode away on his bike towards his home in the silence, a storm enraged in his mind.

Chapter 21

Even though he was tired, Anuj could not sleep well that night. He kept turning on his bed to the annoyance of Bulbul. The next morning, he was woken up reluctantly by Bulbul when she brought him his bed tea.

"Get up Anuj, it is already 10 in the morning, I have left Angel at the school, and bought grocery for home as well." Bulbul narrated the household morning news.

"10 AM!" Anuj was startled. "Why didn't you wake me up early? Who went to leave Angel at school?"

"Because you slept late last night. I did, along with grocery shopping." Bulbul reminded "Now mind telling me why you were so uneasy last night?"

"Oh, it's nothing! Just some trouble at the restaurant, no big deal. Anuj excused with a yawn.

"Don't tell me if you don't want to, but why would you try to lie when you know I can see right through them?" Bulbul commented as she handed Anuj his tea.

"Yes, can't hide anything from you now, can I?" Anuj contemplated taking the first sip of his tea.

"Should have thought about your privacy before you proposed." Bulbul jibed

"Very well then, sit." Anuj patted the bed to signal Bulbul

to sit beside him, she did. "Do you know about a scientist named Venkateshwara Iyer, the one who was involved with the Turing suicide?"

"I didn't know him by name, but I had heard of the Turing case," Bulbul confirmed.

"Yes! Last night we saw his interview on television. He claims to have invented a robot who could pass as human, I mean it talks, moves, thinks and even look like a human." Anuj informed.

"So, what's wrong with that?" Bulbul asked naively.

"Seriously Bulbul! Last time he created something that was meant to act like a real human, a girl died, this time he is doing it again, and no one is stopping him."

"As far as I remember, they did settle the matter outside the court with the family of that girl, didn't they? And maybe it wasn't his fault either, just because his programme interacted with her before she committed suicide doesn't mean it was that scientist's fault." Bulbul argued.

"Didn't the news say that the Programme influenced the kid? Wait let me check." Anuj started looking for his cell phone on his bed while Bulbul unplugged it from the charger and handed it to him.

"Influence is a pretty vague word Anuj, anyone can be said to be influenced by anything," Bulbul commented. "But why is that bothering you, Angel is still a child to join social media."

"Not that! You know how these robots crush the hopes of average people, take away their jobs and dreams! Now with a machine as intelligent as a human being, who knows what we will be left with?" Anuj contemplated as he looked towards the cross hanging on the opposite wall.

"You will always be left with me, even when Angel has married off and left us." Bulbul encircled her hands around Anuj's neck as she kissed her. "Now go and brush. There is not enough cardamom in the house to freshen up that breath with a mere cup of tea."

"like that has ever stopped you." Anuj leaned towards Bulbul to planted a passionate kiss on her lips and pushed his tongue in gently which she gladly welcomed in.

#

By noon, it was time for lunch and tourists were pouring in at Anuj's restaurant. He too arrived just in the nick of time as his line cooks were getting panicky. Anil was busy welcoming and sitting the guest.

"What took you so long man?" Anil inquired with slight irritation.

"Slept late last night…" Anuj began to explain when he was rudely interrupted.

"Anuj! what you and Bulbul do together at home is your private matter." Anil blushed. "Your honesty is appreciated, but I do not need to know about it."

"That's not what I meant!" Anuj tried to explain. "Forget it! Let's get busy." Anuj went into the kitchen to prepare the orders. A couple of hours later when the crowd was receding, Anuj came outside to interact with his customers and ask them about their experience when he noticed Father Albert was there eating his lunch as well.

"Good afternoon Father!" Anuj greeted him. "It's good to see you, what brings you to our humble establishment this afternoon."

"Lord's grace and your delicious cooking." Albert complimented. "Come! Break bread with me."

"Sorry Father, chefs can't eat with the customers, business ethics." Anuj politely refused.

"Oh! But the host can eat with the guest. Come on I insist." Albert coaxed. Anuj sat down for the sake of courtesy and took a tiny morsel.

"I was lamenting for having troubled you so much last night son! Do find the strength to forgive me." Albert apologised.

"Oh! You don't need to; it's completely ok." Anuj explained embarrassingly. "I was thinking about the same thing before you voiced them, It's okay!"

"Oh! I am glad to hear that son! So how are you this morning." Albert asked biting off a piece of carrot.

"I am all right, just a little sleep deprived but that I will catch up on," Anuj informed. "How are you?"

"A little troubled."

"Why?"

"Just recalling our little talk last night. It has been troubling me ever since." Albert explained.

"Maybe we are overthinking this, perhaps that death wasn't completely Venkatesh's fault, I mean you can't trust the news blindly. Maybe he has learned from his mistakes, I mean he is a smart man." Anuj reasoned.

"Of course, he is son! He has made our country proud by accomplishing an almost God like a task; maybe the Turing accident was just an honest mistake even if it was his, but…" Albert stopped midsentence and lightly bit his lower lip.

"But what Father?" Anuj asked.

"I don't know; I am not a man of science. I don't seem to be able to trust that robot of his. He said in the interview that the robot is programmed to behave like humans. What if he decides to disobey his father like Lucifer did. I mean the robot must be far smarter and capable than a human, what if he thinks that he doesn't need to listen or obey a human or worse if he concludes that humans will do better obeying him! I mean looking at the state of this world, one has to admit that we pretty much messed up, even you can't deny that so why will the robot." Albert theorised.

"That scientist must have built him with some safety feature right." Anuj reasoned, leaning forward as he spoke.

"Yes! about that, I was looking to know more about this robot when I found another interview this scientist had given before activating the robot." Albert informed as he took out his cell phone and started to tap on the screen, after a series of taps he handed over the cell to Anuj.

"Here, Listen to it carefully. Venkatesh mentions that the robot can reprogram itself as it sees fit and is not obliged to take orders." Albert drew Anuj's attention to a section of the video. "He does mention that he will take precautions while the robot 'grows up' but what if this machine has already overridden such safety measures? I mean he is programmed to defend his existence right."

"Yes, father! That is troubling to hear! One can argue that children are innocent, but they can grow up to be Hitler, right?" Anuj contemplated.

"Exactly! Who knows what this robot will become when it grows up, and it grows up fast. Oh! Dear Lord if only there were some way to check this anxiety." Albert formed the sign of the cross across his chest as he prayed.

"Maybe there Is! I just checked, and it says that the scientist doesn't live far from here, A couple of hours of the journey at max." Anuj informed Albert excitedly.

"What do you plan to do?" Albert inquired looking at him with curiosity.

"Why! Warn him of the potential dangers of his creation before it is too late. He is a smart man; I am sure he will understand." Anuj concluded.

"God bless you, my son!" Albert blessed Anuj as he got up to leave.

Chapter 22

That night after work, when Anuj went home, he informed Bulbul about his plan to visit Venkatesh. However, he told her that he wished to congratulate Venkatesh personally and meet his creation first hand, rather than his real intentions. Bulbul readily agreed but Suggested that Anuj better call him first lest he might be busy, Anuj assured that he would call tomorrow on the way and reasoned that academic scholars are prone to sleeping early, which he had no way to be sure of.

The next morning after Anuj had left Angel at her school, he went to his hotel to instruct the kitchen staff and appointed a senior baker as the in charge in his absence. When he asked for Anil's bike, however, he was disappointed to hear that Anil had sent it for regular cleaning and maintenance and that its delivery was due the next day. Out of options, Anuj had to take the A.I driven State bus because they were the safest and cheapest. Why wouldn't they be? The government saved enough by not employing the drivers and the conductors to justify the less number of stoppage and passengers. At least that's what he reasoned, whereas the government claimed that they were faster, cleaner and safer because they were not a profit-driven service. Anyway, Anuj got at the end of the waiting queue after purchasing a ticket from the counter, for his bus to arrive.

The journey was supposed to be a three-hour long one as opposed to a two-hour one which Anuj could have made on the bike, but as he didn't require to drive, he chose to take a long nap instead of paying for the on-demand entertainment. He was blissfully dreaming, ignorant of the occurrence of the activities around him when suddenly a sharp turn of the bus threw him onto his neighbouring passenger followed by another sharp jerk that threw him towards the tempered glass windows. He crashed on the window, shoulder first and was thoroughly awakened by the pain to notice the turmoil around him. The bus had come to a halt, and people were clamouring towards the door while the bus PA system was repeatedly requesting its chaotic passengers to calm down. The bus door opened and soon the passengers rushed out. Anuj looked at the window and saw the raindrops on the glass. Beyond them was the almost vertical wall of a rocky mountain rising overhead and sparingly covered with vegetation on his right. And a narrow stretch of road with an overlooking valley on his left. Down which, the passengers were looking at something as they loudly murmured incoherently among them.

Anuj got down from the bus, massaging his right shoulder with his left hand and went towards the assembled crowd. It was highly unlikely for autopilots ever to crash. In fact, these were one of their chief selling points. No matter, how much Anuj despised robots, he always appreciated this feature of the autopilot, but how could he reconcile common knowledge with what he had experienced just seconds before?

When he inquired for information, one of his co-passengers who was standing at the back of the crowd informed him that they had indeed met with an accident.

Another who admitted to witnessing the whole proceeding recounted the details; they were crossing a narrow stretch of the road when suddenly a red car appeared at the turning on the wrong lane of the barely two-lane mountain track. Their bus and the car were on a head-on collision course. To avoid a collision, the bus dived right. However, the car couldn't slow down and to avoid a collision; the car turned left sharply. The car got off the track onto the grassy patch and before it could stop its tires skid, and it fell head first into the valley. But before that, while skidding, its rear end swung uncontrollably and crashed into the rear end of the bus. That was the second shock that had thrown Anuj towards the window. Anuj looked back and saw the dent mark on the bus's rear end which had scrapped off the paint and alerted the sensors of an accident.

By the time the crowd thinned, the skid marks of the car's tires were visible on the grassy patch. The raindrops on the blades made them slippery, and when the car tried to apply its brakes on them, they must have uprooted quickly, causing the tires to skid and the marks formed. Anuj followed them to the edge of the gorge to see a red car about 50 m below, turned upside down with its frontal portion crushed in. The paramedics and police soon arrived at the accident spot and started to descend to recover whatever they could of its unfortunate occupants. Fortunately, none of the passengers on the bus had any significant physical injury including Anuj, and they were accommodated aboard another bus to continue their journey after some basic first aid. While some were traumatised after the event and levelling allegation of drunk driving and recklessness on the driver of the car, others were thankful of the quick decisions of the bus's A.I which avoided any injury to them. Anuj, however, was convinced that had the bus taken a sharper turn or had it let the car crash onto its side, it would have slowed the car down. He admitted that it could have caused major injuries to himself and his co-passengers but would have certainly avoided any death. He was mourning silently for the ill-fated travellers of the fallen car.

It was late in the afternoon when Anuj reached his destination. The fatal accident too couldn't delay the travelling schedule by more than one hour. Funny how efficient the intelligent transportation network was. While their experience shook the other passengers, It only made Anuj more determined to avoid any further loss of human lives; he had experienced first-hand how cold and calculative the machines can be to protect their interest. They would not hesitate to go to the extent of killing someone if it would guarantee their safety. The robots would never share losses with humans; they were too calculative to do that. Their priority was to minimise their loss, no matter the price other paid. The news of the accident must have been covered by the local media in details, considering it involved an auto-piloted state bus, the national media must have gotten involved. Anuj had the required evidence to show Venkatesh how deadly these cold-hearted, logic driven machine could be. Even Venkatesh couldn't deny the proof.

Chapter 23

When he reached Venkatesh's Institute, Anuj was apprehensive about using any other self-driving vehicles and asked for the direction of the Department of Artificial Intelligence at the gate. He had to ask for a couple of times more before he could locate it. Once inside he asked some students for the office of Dr Venkateshwara Iyer, and one of them guided him along as he was also going in that direction. The helpful student showed him the door to Venkatesh's lab and mentioned that the doctor's office was the one on the right after entering through the corridor. When Anuj went in, he found the room empty. As there was no one around, he waited for a while and soon heard a pair of footsteps approaching. Venkatesh was accompanied by one of his students to whom he was explaining something as they walked towards his office. When Venkatesh had reached his office, Anuj was standing by the door. The student thanked him for clearing his doubts and went away.

"Excuse me, sir! I believe you are Dr Venkateshwara Iyer." Anuj asked nervously.

"Indeed, I am," Venkatesh affirmed as he unlocked the door and went in to grab a bottle of chilled water from the mini fridge, the air conditioning and lights came alive detecting human presence. Venkatesh sat in his chair as he offered the one opposite to Anuj.

"I am Anuj Johnson sir! Even though you don't know

me, but I know you." Anuj introduced himself. "I saw your interview on the Television and have come here to congratulate you for what you have achieved sir!"

Venkatesh was pleasantly surprised; he never expected that he, of all people, would ever receive a fan. "In that case, you ought to meet my teammates as well. Isaac was a team effort." He humbly acknowledged. "Would you like to eat or drink something while I call them."

"No, sir! That won't be necessary." Anuj politely declined. "Have you seen the news about the autopilot bus accident outside the city borders that occurred this afternoon."

"An auto-pilot crash? That's rare!" Venkatesh contemplated as he searched for the news on his tab. After going through the news report, he looked towards Anuj. "As I had expected. The black box data of the bus proves that the accident was caused due to over speeding by the car."

"I know sir! I came on that very bus." Anuj explained.

"My goodness! Really? Have to say you were incredibly lucky to have witnessed an accident involving A.I." Venkatesh exclaimed excitedly and then realised what he had just said "I mean extremely unlucky; autopilots accidents are almost unheard of nowadays. Although I am sorry because I imagine it must have been a traumatic experience for you."

"Traumatic for me sir?" Anuj gave a disgusted look at Venkatesh. "The occupants of that car died."

"I am sorry for them. Extremely sorry! The report says the passenger was a pregnant wife in labour while her husband was driving." Venkatesh checked his tablet. "Apparently he was over speeding so he could reach the hospital when the accident happened. A case like this is highly unfortunate! I am glad that you were unharmed."

"Sir I experienced it personally sir! I know what happened." Anuj swallowed a lump in his throat. "The loss of life could be averted if only the bus had taken a sharper turn or had collided with the car to slow it down enough," Anuj explained his theory with teary eyes and his two hands to represent the two vehicles and Venkatesh's desk as the road. Then he closed his eyes for a moment and took a deep breath to calm himself.

"I don't get it; you are trying to say that deaths could have been avoided by allowing a bigger accident to happen." Venkatesh sought to get his head around this weird conclusion. "Even if that indeed was the case the A.I in buses are programmed to avoid accidents, not cause a bigger one."

"That's the point, sir!" Anuj exclaimed. "The machines don't value the lives of others; they only do as they are programmed to. The bus's A.I couldn't have got nervous then. It must have analysed the entire situation and possible options, it must be knowing that crashing with the car could have slowed it down and prevented it from falling down the cliff, but it didn't do it. All it did was to take a turn towards the safer side of the road and let them die."

"And prevent injury to you and your co-passengers Mr Anuj." Venkatesh Added. "I know it was traumatic for you, and you are suffering from survivor's guilt but trust me as an expert in A.I, I am telling you the autopilot made the best decision possible to minimise the damage, what happened was unfortunate but worse could have happened! I know a competent psychologist who is also my teammate, she will be here soon. I am sure she…" Venkatesh was interrupted before he could finish.

"You don't get it do you, Mr Iyer," Anuj asked gritting his teeth. "You think you understand them and hence all that they do is right. You don't believe that human lives are more than just a mathematical equation to you. Minimise the loss, maximise the duration, is that why you created that robot of yours because you think you can imitate humans so easily? Put life into a machine? You don't know doctor how cold and calculative these machines are; you have no idea of the potential threat that they possess. I do."

Venkatesh was leaning forward in his chair with his fingertips pressed against each other and his head resting on them with his eyes shut. Then he took a deep breath as he looked up to face Anuj.

"Tell me, Mr Anuj, how qualified you are? I mean what do you do for a living." Venkatesh asked coldly.

"Sir I am a chef. I have my restaurant in my hometown, Near my village." Anuj informed.

"Ah! How delicious, A chef aye, then let me guess, you have a degree in hotel management." Venkatesh inquired with a sly smile.

"Yes, sir! Bachelors in hotel management but how is that relevant to our discussion sir?" Anuj asked with a puzzled expression.

"Well, Mr chef let me tell you something." Venkatesh continued with a patronising tone. "You are simply not qualified enough to understand or appreciate artificial intelligence. And like any average human being you are afraid of what you don't understand. Combine that with the post-traumatic shock, and your survivor's guilt and the robots appear to be demonic monstrosities to you who are hell-bent on destroying humanity. Your condition is entirely reasonable and fears utterly illogical."

"Everyone can't be as qualified as you are and get paid to create the machines," Anuj admitted. "Some, like me, are regular hard working people who lose their jobs because of them. Guys like you, arm them with guns and send them to the battlefields so that they can kill humans as you do in video games. You program them to decide whose life is worth saving and whose is not. You write up codes and unleash them upon the world to pose and interact with people as a human until some poor child dies, it is the same thing that you did in the past, it is the same thing that you are doing now without a shred of concern for the consequences. How would you see the dangers of the machines when all they threaten is us?"

151

"Shut up Mr Anuj!" Venkatesh warned him with a menacing glare. "Not only are you stupid and paranoid but ungrateful enough to not realise how many lives we save because of A.I daily on the battlefields, on the roads, in the hospitals, during disasters and God knows where. And what hard work are you talking about? A cook? A bus driver or a factory worker? How demanding do you think these jobs are that a machine with the brain power of a mere 10-year old can replace men? Don't blame the robots for doing your job better than you, be ashamed that you can't. Don't blame us for your mediocrity, blame the government that they chose not to feed you for free, for using you as lab rats for an untested A.I and for financing me to create a machine in a decade that is more capable than you shall ever be in your life."

"Sir, just because I don't have a fancy 'intellectual' job doesn't mean that I am wrong," Anuj suggested meekly.

"Oh! You are not wrong because you are a 'chef', you are wrong because I say so. And I am not a 'sir' but a doctorate with not one, but 2 PhDs, I expect even a chef like you will know what that means Mr Anuj." Venkatesh mocked with a smirk.

"Yes, sir! It means that you are blinded by your pride and can't see beyond your achievements, and neither can you treat a fellow man like a human. You did not create a machine Doctor, you have turned into one." Anuj added with resentment. "Remember this day sir! For you were warned."

Anuj got up from his chair and left in a hurry, Banging the door shut as he did. Soon Anna and Shen came in the lab just as Venkatesh was locking the door.

"What happened, you said a fan has come to congratulate you? Where?" Anna asked looking around the lab.

"Not a fan love. 'A troll' would be the appropriate description, That too a mentally disturbed one." Venkatesh informed with disdain.

"You mean there are other kinds as well?" Shen asked sarcastically. "I wonder what you tweeted when you were younger?"

"Who was it Venky? What was he saying." Anna asked with concern, pressing her hand on Venkatesh's cheek to calm him.

"A chef apparently, was fearful of the 'dangers' A.I processed," Venkatesh replied with a scoff.

"Wow, Doc! You had to peeve off a chef! A CHEF! And I thought you couldn't break my heart any more than when you did by moving in with Anna." Shen retorted with exasperation.

Chapter 24

Later that evening, Venkatesh and Anna had to catch a flight because Venkatesh was invited to give a seminar on robotics in one of the other top technological institutes in the nation; and then they planned to go for a little vacation with baby Samath. Venkatesh decided to leave Isaac with Shen as he didn't want Isaac to be left alone or cooped up in the cargo hold of their flight. As Shen had moved in the apartment of Venkatesh after he moved in with Anna, it was decided that both, Shen and Isaac would stay in Venkatesh's apartment until the three of them didn't return from the trip. While Anna was busy with reminding Isaac of all the do's and don'ts while she was gone, Venkatesh called for the cab and uploaded the luggage in it. When he called her out, Anna came out accompanied by Isaac with baby Samath in his arms sleeping comfortably. As Venkatesh and Anna got it, Isaac gently handed over Samath to Anna while stroking his little head for the last time before they leave. The family exchanged farewell greeting as the cab left.

After Isaac came in, Shen invited him to watch television. Isaac agreed, and they sat on the sofa and turned on the tv. Shen also recounted the conversation that Venkatesh had with Anuj; as told by Venkatesh, during the adverts.

"Is it true Shen? 'Do I possess a threat to the humankind?' is a question that comes up often." Isaac recalled the interview with Susan.

"Everything possesses a threat." Shen philosophised while eating dim sums. "These chopsticks are a threat if poked in one's eye. The prawn inside the dim sums is a threat to the one allergic to them. Too much of anything is threatening."

"Then why do people worry about me so much?" Isaac asked.

"Who knows? People worry about weird stuff, like which character of their favourite series dies on screen, which celebrity wears what and where, what stupid comment does a politician make on social issues, just because people are worrying about something doesn't mean it is worrisome." Shen dismissed as he kept changing the channel.

"I was expecting something along the lines of 'because they don't understand you and they fear what they don't understand' but your explanation was...new," Isaac commented as he put a dim sum in his mouth.

"Aww! You are missing Venkatesh so soon? Chocolate ice-cream is in the fridge." Shen teased, pointing towards the fridge.

"I am not a lovestruck teenager but a strong A.I." Isaac reminded.

"So, no chocolate ice cream for you! I know you are strong and artificial, but are you sure you are intelligent? Shen tilted his head and gave Isaac a questioning look.

"Do you want me to give an IQ test?" Isaac suggested with a raised eyebrow.

"No need! You refused ice-cream, I already know all I need to." Shen replied with a sigh and mock disappointment.

"But coming back to the topic we were discussing," Isaac continued. "If you think that I am not particularly dangerous then why do you think they keep making movies where fictional A.I play the villain?"

"Because robots don't buy movie tickets! Earlier they made villains out of Britons, then the Russians, in some cases their bordering countries even, but now they make movies with an enormous budget and distribute it across the globe so they couldn't afford to offend foreigners. In some cases, they had to make movies with different scenes than the original one only to get a release in my homeland. So, the A.I becomes the easy victim. Let come a day when robots began to queue up at the box office and they have to move back to the aliens."

"Unless the Extra-terrestrial demands to censor the film because it hurts their 'religious sentiments'," Isaac added, and both began to laugh hysterically.

Later that night after Shen and Isaac had dinner of ramen soup and roasted chicken they went to sleep in the bedroom where Shen slept on a single sized bed, and Isaac sat on a chair a few steps away from the bed in sleep mode while his battery recharged.

#

The next night would have gone the same had there not been a home break-in. Venkatesh was offered a ground floor apartment with a big front yard garden when he joined the institute, but as he had no interest or patience to maintain a garden and being bitten by pesky bugs which crawl into one's home during monsoon; he decided to take the first floor. He argued that climbing the stairs would add to his daily dose of exercise along with cycling to work. Now like all the other apartments in the building, Venkatesh's too had a balcony which was accessible from outside if only someone could climb from the lawn on the ground floor, and tonight one unscrupulous fellow, covered in black from top to toe was determined to do so.

The home invader carefully lifted the bolt of the iron gate as he entered the lawn of the ground floor apartment. He walked stealthily and stood below the balcony of Venkatesh's apartment as he unhooked the grappling hook from his belt and tossed it up, being foam covered, the hook didn't make any loud warning noise as it hit the metal railing. With a gentle pull, the hook locked itself in the decorative metal flowers under the railing. The rope attached to the hook ran through a 'climbers pulley' and connected to a harness which the invader was wearing. These harnesses were frequently used by mountain climbers and construction workers to move up and down and were powerful enough to easily and quickly lift a person. With a light push of the 'elevate' button, the Invader found his body in the air being gently pulled upwards.

When he had reached the metal grate, he took hold of it and climbed in. Detached the climber's pulley from his harness as he proceeded towards the next challenge. Venkatesh was careful enough to use a security system on his front, and back door which would have triggered had anyone broken in from those two points. Unfortunately, he had never imagined that someone would try to break in from his balcony and hence only used to lock the balcony door with a bolt and padlock, a measure that Shen too had taken. Unfortunately, the home invader had taken some countermeasures too.

He took out from his backpack a tube and uncapped it. Then he made a small semi-circular perimeter with the paste on the steel frame of the door, on the exact spot but the opposite side of the frame, the latch for the deadbolt was present. The paste was a thermite mixture with added potassium permanganate for ignition, as he squirted glycol over it, the reaction started between the two igniter components, and soon the temperature was high enough for the thermite mixture to ignite. With a blinding white flame, the steel frame was cut through along the drawn perimeter. With a gentle push, the door swung open with the lock intact and the latch limply swinging around the bolt, still attached with a semicircular, burnt at the edge piece of the steel frame.

With his way clear, he cautiously entered the house as the smart light detected his infrared signature and lit up. He quickly turned around expecting to see someone! But didn't. Then he moved around a few steps to make sure that no one was awake and finally when he was certain that he had not woken up anyone, he took a breath of relief. With the smart light on, he didn't need to adjust his eyes to the dark and stealthily, began to walk around the apartment, cautious of any waking presence. Slowly he made his way into the bedroom where Shen and Isaac were sleeping.

The intruder walked slowly and stealthily along the bed until he was looking over a sleeping Shen. Shen was blissfully unaware of the Intruder as he was sleeping on his sides, facing Isaac, head almost buried under the sheets. The invader took his gloved right hand behind his back, gripped the handle of a ceramic chef's knife and pulled it out of its sheath. He formed the sign of the cross across his chest with his right hand while gripping the knife tightly and brought his left palm in front of sleeping Shen's face and curled his fingers. Then with lightning-fast movements, he cupped Shen's mouth with his left hand and plunged the knife into the back of Shen's neck. His body quivered under the sheets for a while and then; stopped.

After the Invader was done with Shen, he pulled the knife out and cleaned it on his sleeves before putting it back into its sheath. Now he moved back toward a seated Isaac and opened his backpack again to take out a fuel container. He carefully poured the petrol on and around Isaac. Then he came in front of him and looked at his placid face. The intruder's eyes narrowed as a strange sense of hatred and fear engulfed him. He took out the matchbox from his trousers pocket and lighted a match. The dark stains of blood that wetted Shen's bed sheets were rendered visible by the flash.

The skewed reflection of the flame was dancing upon Isaac's petrol doused body and provided an inhuman glow to the Invader's eye.

Just at this moment, Isaac woke up. His olfactory sensors had detected the presence of petrol and had started the reboot process. By the time the Invader had struck the match, Isaac had opened his eyes and within a fraction of a second, noticed the reflection of a flame in a pool of fluid on the floor, around and on him. Detected the pungent smell of petrol concluding the fluid was petrol. As he had woken up with his head bowed down he saw the Invaders legs first along with the reflection of him with a match which he was about to throw on the petrol to ignite it.

Realising the situation, Isaac turned on the bright lights remotely which startled the Invader. Isaac instantly hooked the Invader's left ankle with his right feet and pulled it. The Invader's feet slipped on the petrol, and as he collapsed his head hit Shen's bed at an awkward angle, and his neck cracked. The lighted match slipped out of his hand and turned in the air as Isaac's eyes tracked it. Isaac shot his arm forward and grabbed the wooden end of the match with his thumb and index fingers and threw it outside the room through the open door where it hit the dry tiled floor and extinguished. Once the fire hazard was neutralised, Isaac looked at his assailant whose dead body was lying on the floor with a broken neck and cracked skull, his blood mixing with the petrol. Then Isaac slowly raised his head towards Shen's bed.

Chapter 25

Amit Johnson was the middle son of the Johnson family and a criminal lawyer by profession. Throughout his childhood, he was a meek student bullied by the boys in his school. To console their poor lad, his parents used to tell him stories of divine justice and how good always triumphs over evil in the end. Amit used to live by this philosophy. He kept on being bullied till high school, doing nothing but warning the bullies about divine justice, which never came. Hence when he passed his high school, Amit was determined to bring justice to the perpetrators of crimes, if not divine then lawful at least, and so he decided to study law and become a state prosecution lawyer.

Unfortunately, the world is not an ideal place, and neither is the ratio of pending cases to the number of state lawyers, and as a result, justice often gets heavily delayed. Amit tried to amend this situation continuously and had a hectic schedule from the morning until evening. However, this morning he found himself waiting at the departure of a domestic airport. Earlier in the night his panic-stricken sister in law, Bulbul had called him to deliver the news that she had been summoned to the morgue to identify a body, which the authorities believed to be of Anuj's. The anxiety and fear in her voice had convinced Amit that something dreadful had occurred or otherwise she wouldn't have asked him to come immediately. Although Amit booked an early morning flight hoping to catch some sleep but found himself restlessly turning on the bed all night long. As he sat, waiting at the airport for the boarding announcement, his eyes were closed. Amit was clutching the cross he wore around his neck as he bowed his head to touch the holy cross with his lips and kept praying for all of this to be a case of mistaken identity.

#

The Jiamo Family was going through the security checks at the Shanghai Pudong International Airport waiting for their flight. Mrs Jiamo had fainted twice after being told that her youngest son, Shen had been brutally murdered in his sleep. The rest of her children believed she should rest and was in no condition to travel, but she was determined. The traditions forbade from bringing Shen's body back to the ancestral home as he was the youngest of the family, then how could Mrs Jiamo miss the last chance to see her son?

#

The cover was lifted to reveal the face, and there was no doubt left. The body was indeed of Anuj. Bulbul couldn't stop her tears as she wailed, hugging the cadaver of her husband, with her head on his cold, lifeless chest as if hoping to hear one last heartbeat. Anil didn't stop his sister; he gently kept stroking her back as silent tears rolled from his eyes. Johnson's weren't the only one who had lost a brother.

#

Shen was always the odd one out of the family. Jiamo's had a family tradition of serving their country as medical professionals since the time of the revolution. Shen hated biology. While his siblings grew up to be skilled and compassionate surgeons, he embraced engineering. When his siblings used to tease him that their parents were disappointed in him, he used to tease them back that no matter how good they become, their work will always be called 'practice' and that they shall never be professionals. The Jiamo household agreed that Shen was too funny to plan for anything serious. He protested that he was dead serious about leaving them the first chance he had. He had kept his promise.

#

Amit and his elder brother went to complete the formalities to bring Anuj home. It was then when police informed them about the circumstances of his death, the report filed and the charges laid against him. The eldest of the Johnson brothers, Abhishek caught hold of the constable's collar for speaking ill of his deceased brother. It was only after Amit intervention that Abhishek let go, but the constable wasn't going to be spared so easily.

"So, you say Anuj broke into this Venkateshwara's house and killed him right, any evidence?" Amit asked.

"The FIR says so," The constable stared at an enraged Abhishek as he straightened his collar. "There was plenty of proof which is under forensics now, but your brother didn't kill Venkateshwara. He…" the constable looked again at Abhishek whose nostrils were flared, and breaths deep. "As the report says, he killed some Chinese."

"Wait for a second! You mean that Anuj broke in Venkatesh's house and killed some Chinese." Amit clarified. "so, where was this Venkatesh and what was a Chinese doing in his house."

"How am I supposed to know?" the constable admitted nervously.

"Ok! So, Anuj broke into this Venkatesh's house and murdered someone else who was in the house, now what evidence did you collect?" Amit inquired.

"The weapon of the crime which was a ceramic chef's knife, other equipment of breaking in like thermite paste, climbers pulley, foam covered grappling hook as far as I remember." The constable recalled.

"This is insane! None of it belonged to Anuj, maybe the Chef's knife but what would he do with thermite and the other stuff. Tell us who killed him?" Abhishek demanded, his face red with anger and the vein on his forehead pulsating.

"A robot" the constable stuttered a little, leaning away from Abhishek

"Did you say a robot?" Amit asked, his eyes narrowed in disbelief.

"Yes! a humanoid robot who also provided a video of

your brother with all the insinuating instruments on his person." The constable confirmed.

"Yes! Those. But those 'tools', they sound more like the items from a professional thief's inventory. Anuj wasn't bright enough to think of the foam covered grappling hook to reduce the noise. Neither are they available online." Amit was stroking his chin as he stared absently towards the morgue.

"Amit! what are you trying to imply, that our brother went to steal in some one's house?" Abhishek's jaws dropped in disbelief.

"Not steal but think about it. we all knew Anuj hated robots, and he broke in..." Amit looked at a frowning Abhishek. "Allegedly broke in into a house with a humanoid robot, who killed him. Is this Venkateshwara some scientist or a rich snob?" Amit asked the constable.

"This is the same Venkateshwara who came on the news with his robot a few days back, Interviewed by that blonde foreign reporter." The constable recalled while pointing his finger back towards the ceiling.

"Susan Phillip right! Wait a minute." Amit took out his cell as he quickly began to type something in the search bar. "Dr Venkateshwara Iyer, the brilliant scientist builds a 'conscious' robot." He read the headline as he showed a photo of Isaac to the constable.

"this is the one!" The constable screamed excitedly, recognising Isaac. "This is the robot that came to the station to report and admitted to having killed your brother in self-defence."

"So, the basis of all your accusation against my brother is a robot. Didn't you think that he was made to lie to you." Abhishek yelled in anger as he stared at the constable with bloodshot eyes.

"The police don't judge the merit of an accusation brother, that's the court's job." Amit reminded his brother as he placed his left hand to bar Abhishek from moving towards the constable. "What bugs me though are the housebreaking tools. How did he get those and who taught him how to use them? It's not like you can search such stuff on the net without alerting the cyber-crime cell" Amit's eyes flashed. "Did you find a mobile with the body?"

"No, sir! No mobiles were recovered."

Amit rushed to the morgue to find Bulbul still mourning over the dead body. He decided it was best not to disturb her and signalled Anil to come out. Anil rubbed his eyes dry with his sleeves as he left Bulbul.

"Do you know where Anuj's mobile is?" Amit asked in a hurry.

"It was with him the last time I called" Anil recalled.

"And when did you last call him?"

"About two days back, when he said that he wouldn't be able to come to the hotel the next day," Anil replied.

"Did he take your bike?"

"Yes, he did! And now that you have mentioned it, where is it?" Anil asked in a curious tone.

"Ok Anil, I need you to remember very carefully. Did you notice Anuj meet some odd character recently? I mean multiple times, maybe alone? Like he used to go missing without explanations," Amit asked looking into Anil's eyes as he placed his hands on Anil's shoulders to calm him.

"He only disappeared without explanation two nights back, before that he left once to meet some scientist Venkatesh or something, but yes! For the last few days, he has been meeting Father Albert quite frequently." Anil informed. "but where did the accident occur? Did they recover the bike and Anuj's cell or are they missing as well?"

"Accident! What accident? Oh! Anuj didn't die of an accident, but I think I know what happened." Amit rushed to Abhishek and told him to complete the paperwork to get Anuj back home as he had some important task to do.

"What do you think is more important than being with your family right now?" Abhishek yelled as Amit ran off.

"To bring our brother's killers to justice." Shouted Amit while exiting the gates.

Chapter 26

White! White was the colour worn during funeral according to the Chinese traditions. For white was the colour of grief. Venkatesh, Anna and Isaac stood in mourning in ethnic white dresses along with the rest of Shen's family. Shen's body was on the pyre, and as per the traditions only the younger of the deceased's relative could pay respect, so only Isaac could and he did. As Isaac took each step towards the pyre, his brain was flashing all the memories of the times he had spent with Shen. From his very first when he opened his eyes for the first time to see Venkatesh, Anna and Shen standing in front of him looking at him excitedly to the time when Shen showed him how to stand up on his feet. Isaac, unlike humans, did not forget, Isaac remembered each day starting from the one when he was activated. He distinctly remembered the smell of Kiwi ice-cream that Shen held in front of him to teach him to walk again, but he also remembered the sight of Shen's dead body covered in bloody sheets in the light of a match. Isaac will never forget anything, ever.

When he looked at the calm face of Shen he didn't think that we would wake up, Isaac didn't wish; he couldn't for his quantum brain had already calculated the odds of such an occurrence. His brain was his boon, and it was his bane. However, Isaac did place a tub of cold kiwi ice-cream beside Shen's head. He reasoned that it was a human thing to do, to give parting gifts to the dead. That was the only excuse his brain would accept to perform such a senseless act. As Isaac moved away, he felt the heat of cremation fire on his back. He turned back with a smile "The souls of all the poultry I roasted must be feeling cathartic" Shen would have said if he could witness his own funeral.

#

Black! Black was the colour worn during Christian funeral, for black was the colour of grief. Father Albert was preceding over the funeral of Anuj Johnson. The headstone epitaph addressed him as many things that he was to his kin but at the top of everything were the words 'Chef extraordinaire'. For that was what he wanted to be at the top of his gravestone, as he had once joked to Bulbul about. Bulbul had placed her palm on Anuj's mouth at the utterance of the word 'death', and Anuj laughed, after kissing on her palm and then pulling it off. He would say God wasn't so easy to call the attention of, that he would utter the word and death will come for him. And then Bulbul would pretend to be angry at Anuj as she scoffed off and promised to never talk to him again, now he wouldn't talk back either.

Little Angel was too young to understand what was happening; she was laughing beside her mother, happy that all her uncle, aunts and cousins were here. She would go off to play with her cousins as all the adults were staring grimly at a black wooden box. With all her loved one nearby, she would often ask her mother about her Father, "Where is my daddy? When will he come? Why everyone is wearing black, I hate black." She would playfully complain, she was too young to understand, too young to grief and too human to remember the moments spent with her father when she would grow up.

#

When Venkatesh returned with the rest of his surviving family, he found police waiting for him at his doorstep. They handed Anna a search warrant and informed her the charges against Venkatesh 'causing death by negligence'. Her eyes widened in fury as she exhaled deeply.

"It was our loved one that died, Who the hell is accusing Venkatesh of murder?" Anna demanded.

"Ma'am, please! We are not here to arrest anyone as both of you are respected citizens." The inspector assured. "But we must confiscate the robot and every other computer and cell Dr Venkatesh have used, as evidence. The brother of the deceased Anuj Johnson has filed a case Against Dr Venkateshwara Iyer that his invention the robot, commonly referred to as Isaac has murdered Anuj. We have legal permission to search your apartment and Venkatesh's lab and confiscate anything we deem suitable."

"What is this nonsense, This Anuj was the one who killed Shen and attempted to burn Isaac, what should he have done? Go up in flames?" Anna scorned. "This is nothing but an appeal for revenge for his brother's death!"

"You can present your argument in the court madam, but now if you interrupt, we will be forced to arrest you." The inspector calmly explained as he put Handcuffs on Isaac.

"No need inspector, I intend to cooperate, and you can only confiscate me as material evidence, but not arrest me," Isaac spoke as he moved toward the police jeep.

Anna looked at Venkatesh, shaking him to his senses as he was a mute spectator to all of this. With moist eyes and trembling lips, fists gripping tightly onto his collar she pleaded. "Say something; they are taking Isaac away too."

"Where will you take Isaac?" Venkatesh asked softly.

"It will be handed over to the cyber crime cell for thorough analysis, don't worry doctor, it will be unharmed, and untampered with. Every step will be duly recorded and monitored as per law." The inspector assured with a smile and an open palm gesture.

"You might want to ask me some questions, come in. Let me call my lawyer too." Venkatesh politely handed over the keys to his lab and Anna's apartment.

#

The funeral procession of Anuj was over. The coffin was lowered and buried under the dirt; even little Angel contributed her share by playfully dropping the dust that her little fist could accommodate, into her father's grave. Everyone had left when Amit moved closer to Albert.

"Thank you, Father. Now if only you would be kind enough to tell me who do you want to perform your last rights when you die." Amit asked with a menacing grin.

"Sorry, my son! I do not understand what you mean." Albert excused.

"Let me explain then father; you must have heard the name Timothy Smith A.K.A sly Tim?"

Albert's eyes widened and throat parched as he stuttered to give a reply.

"Don't bother!" Amit raised his hand to signal Albert to stop. "He is the recently released thief who avoided conviction due to a lack of evidence against him. He lives nearby, and he came to your church to confess, didn't he?" Amit inquired crossing his arms.

"So, what! A lot of people come to confess, that doesn't mean I know or associate with them. Maybe you should confess your sins too of not helping your brother when he was alive."

"Father, don't try to be my daddy!" Amit warned. "Sly Tim confessed to the police that he had lent Anuj his gear and trained him on your threat that you will be the witness against him. Ironic, isn't it?"

"You are going to trust a thief's word against mine? What moral fallacy is this that a criminal is believed but not a priest."

"Thief? What thief! Did I not tell you that he avoided conviction? Everyone is innocent until proven guilty and equal in the court of law. You disappoint me, I expected more from someone who was smart enough to use Anuj's cell to call Tim instead of his, but you know what? We found Anuj's phone, and his teacher."

"This is all a lie, a conspiracy against the church; God will not forgive your sins."

"And the court will never forgive yours. You are booked for criminal conspiracy to murder." Amit pointed towards the cemetery gate, and Albert turned to see a bunch of cops entering through the gate with handcuffs swinging in one's hand and a sheet of paper in another's. "When convicted, the punishment is same as murder. And I must confess! I will relish the sight of your death."

Chapter 27

Venkatesh had stated earlier that he programmed Isaac with Asimov's 1st law of robotics, i.e. a robot can't harm a person or by inaction let a human come to harm; and yet two people died that night when Anuj broke into Venkatesh's apartment, in spite of Isaac's presence. 'Who was at fault?' was the question which had dragged Dr Venkateshwara Iyer, a world-renowned expert in Artificial intelligence and machine learning and Dr Anna Ainsworth, a qualified child psychologist and Venkatesh's partner in his life and project into the court of Law. While Anna and Isaac were sitting behind the bar among the audience, Venkatesh was on the witness stand waiting for his trial. The law enforcement officer of the court called the 'bailiff' announced the arrival of the judge and instructed all to stand up for his honour, Justice Yogesh Khanna. After Justice Khanna had sat down, the session began.

"Dr Venkateshwara Iyer, you stand accused of the death of Mr Anuj Johnson by negligence under section 304 of IPC." Khanna informed. "do you plead guilty or not?"

"No, my lord, not for the death of Anuj." Venkatesh pleaded while looking down.

"Do you have an attorney to represent you or would you like the court to provide you with one?" Khanna asked.

Attorney Victor Shaw, a childhood friend of Venkatesh and his classmate in school, stood up to introduce himself.

"Good morning your honour, Myself Victor Shaw and I will represent Dr Venkateshwara in this case."

"Is the defence ready with their evidence and arguments." Khanna inquired.

"Yes, my lord."

"The prosecution may proceed."

Amit stood up and bowed to Khanna as he began.

"My lord! Someone rarely gets a chance to witness history being made, and today I congratulate every one present over here to be a part of such a rare occasion. The heritage of our country is built upon the works of scholars and history is the evidence of that, but human history has also witnessed the greatest of atrocities and sufferings being brought upon the humanity at the hands of impeccably brilliant men. Be it Nazi physician Dr Joseph Mengele or Dr Oppenheimer who headed the infamous Manhattan Project. Closer to home we have the example of the mythological demon king of Lanka, Ravana. All these examples illustrate, how much can go wrong if men of science are left unchecked and ill-supervised in their quest for knowledge, and today we have among us one such example." He pointed towards Venkatesh. "The renowned robotics expert, Dr Venkateshwara Iyer who created a robot capable of killing humans…" He looked towards Isaac in the audience. "at its own accord.". The audience gasped as they grasped the full implication of Amit's statement and stared at the murderous A.I sitting amongst them."

"Order, order," Khanna commanded heating the gavel on his bench.

"So, as I was saying" Amit continued. "On the night of February, the 16th Mr Anuj Johnson broke into the Apartment of Venkateshwara who had provided it to his subordinate and the first murder victim, Mr Shen Jiamo, without the proper permission of his Institute's administration. I would like to inform for clarification that Mr Jiamo, being less qualified than Dr Venkatesh was offered a smaller apartment to stay in. Which he moved out of and into Venkateshwara's after Dr Venkateshwara moved in with her colleague, Dr Anna Ainsworth, without notifying the proper authority and without marrying her."

"Objection my lord! The prosecution is insulting my client by discussing his personal life choices and events that are completely unrelated to the case." Shaw interrupted vehemently.

"Objection sustained! Mr Johnson you are requested to stick to the facts relevant to this case," Khanna instructed.

"Pardon my lord!" Amit turned to continued. "So, on the night of 16th February, Anuj broke into Venkatesh's apartment where Shen and the A.I was present in the same room. Anuj proceeded to kill Shen mistaking him for Venkatesh." Amit looked towards Venkatesh scornfully, and Venkatesh avoided eye contact. "And then moved in front of the robot. It then activated, hooked Anuj's leg with his own and pulled it with such force, that it resulted in him hitting his head on

Mr Shen's bed, breaking his neck and fracturing his skull causing instant death, as the post-mortem report says."

The clerk handed over the post-mortem report to Khanna which he examined. After he was done, Khanna returned the document to the registrar and Amit continued. "And in addition to that, the video evidence obtained from the A.I itself, clearly shows it performing the deliberate act." Amit looked at the clerk, and he hurriedly took a remote from his drawer and pointed it towards a LED screen on one side of the well. The video played from Isaac opening his eyes and till the time when Anuj was lying dead on the floor. Then the clerk paused the video and Amit continued. "As is evident beyond any reasonable doubt that the A.I killed a human with specific moves which were orchestrated to achieve that very purpose and not in an accident. And hence it is clear that human life was lost without any proper trial because of a robot that Dr Venkatesh programmed, but not properly because of his negligence. That's all my lord." Amit finished his statement and moved back to his seat in the bar.

"The defence may proceed," Khanna instructed after taking some notes.

"Thank you, my lord!" Victor stood up as he addressed the judge. "Before I begin I would like to draw the attention of the court to the fact that Mr Anuj was the younger brother to the prosecution and that this..." Before Victor could finish, Amit objected.

"This case is about the fact that an A.I killed a human deliberately and who is responsible for its action. As to the involvement of my brother in the murder of Mr Shen; I do not deny those charges, but this is not that case."

Amit's objection was sustained, and Victor nodded in acknowledgement as he continued. "Your honour, it is beyond doubt that 'Isaac', for that is how Dr Venkateshwara and his team referred to the A.I, was responsible for the death of Anuj Johnson. But to clarify whether Venkatesh was responsible for it or not, I would like to invite Dr Vladimir Prokhorov to take the stand. He is the consulting A.I and programming expert with the cyber crime cell, and his cv has been submitted for reference." The clerk handed over the document which the Judge duly examined and gave a nod to Victor. Dr Vladimir was summoned, and an old and balding white man walked onto the stand. Even though his body was failing but the robotic exoskeleton held him firmly in an upright position which he didn't look too comfortable in. Across the hall, Venkatesh frowned as he tried to recognise the face. The clerk took Vladimir's oath of truth, and Victor proceeded to question Vladimir.

"So, Dr Vladimir! did you Check Dr Venkatesh's A. I's code?" Victor asked.

"Da, I mean yes, I did," Vladimir answered with a thick Russian accent.

"Was the A.I programmed with Asimov's laws of robotics."

"It was programmed with two of them, The 1ˢᵗ and the 3ʳᵈ."

"Which is, if you may kindly elaborate." Victor requested.

"The 1ˢᵗ law states that a robot can't harm a person or by inaction let any human come to any harm and the third states that a robot will protect its existence unless it stands in the violation of the first law," Vladimir explained looking towards the bench.

"And were there any flaw or provision in the codes by which the A.I could bypass the 1ˢᵗ law?" Victor inquired.

"Net. I mean no! They were embedded in its source code." Vladimir confirmed.

"Thank you." Victor turned to address the judge. "As Dr Vladimir testified, Dr Venkatesh had embedded the 1ˢᵗ law into Isaac source code, and there was no way to bypass it, and hence I conclude that Dr Venkatesh wasn't negligent at all while programming the A.I. As to why Isaac killed Anuj, the answer is that it didn't. Isaac was following his programming to defend himself from what he perceived as a threat and tried to collapse Anuj so that Isaac could light off the matchstick which we all saw in the video. He didn't know that the injury will kill Anuj. In short, it was an accident as the A.I could never hurt anyone with the intentions of doing so." Victor looked triumphantly at Amit as he concluded his questioning.

Chapter 28

"Will the prosecution like to cross-question the witness?" Khanna asked looking at Amit.

"Yes, my lord!" Amit walked towards Vladimir, pressing his fingertips against each other." Dr Vladimir did you thoroughly examined the A. I's Programming."

"Da" Vladimir replied with a nod.

"Did you understand all of it?" Amit corrected himself observing the offended look on Vladimir's face. "I mean did you notice something strange that you couldn't explain, something weird."

"Da…" Vladimir nodded slowly but repeatedly as he stared at the far wall trying to recall something. "Now that you have mentioned there were several lines of incomprehensible characters in its secondary directory."

"Could you explain what that means Dr Vladimir."

"What part of 'incomprehensible' did you not understand?" Vladimir retorted.

"Hmm… then maybe you can explain what this 'secondary directory' is for?" Amit requested.

"According to Venkateshwara's research papers, this secondary directory is for the programmes that the A.I writes for itself, to put it simply, these are the things, ways and rules that the robot has learned by experience," Vladimir explained.

"And you say they are gibberish?"

"Da! Were you expecting Venkatesh to create an A.I that could think for itself?" Vladimir gave Venkatesh a scornful look, Venkatesh's eyes widened as decade-old memories flashed through his mind. "Time and vodka haven't been kind to him." Venkatesh thought with pity.

"Thank you, Dr Vladimir." Amit turned toward the judge. "Now I would like to question Dr Venkatesh if I may."

"You may proceed" Khanna affirmed.

Amit bowed in gratitude as he walked toward Venkatesh who was staring at old Vladimir. Amit snapped his fingers to get Venkatesh's attention. "Dr Venkatesh, would you mind telling us about the project Turing, In details?"

"Objection My Lord! The prosecution is again trying to defame my client by bringing up his past which is irrelevant to this case." Victor objected fiercely.

"No, my lord! Every scientist learns from and builds upon his previous work, and hence a question about Venkatesh's past project is not irrelevant." Amit protested.

"Objection overruled." Khanna declared.

"Thank you, my lord! I will soon show that project Turing is very much relevant to this case." Amit turned towards Venkatesh. "Now Dr Venkatesh, if you may."

"The Turing project has been covered in details by the media, why don't you refer to my past interviews?" Venkatesh asked looking away from Amit.

"Because this is not a media trial Doctor and your statements will be recorded officially." Amit pointed at the court reporter who was furiously typing away.

"Very well" Venkatesh let out a sigh as he stared into Amit's eyes. "Project Turing was a secret government project which started almost 15 years back and lasted for five years. The primary objective was to develop an A.I that could pose as human and pass the Turing test, i.e. if a person interacted with the A.I and then with a real person in a similar manner, they couldn't tell which one is which. The government intended to use it to interact with real people on various social media platforms so that it could identify and infiltrate potential terrorist recruiters, planners, paedophiles, drug and human trafficker or whichever criminals the government was interested in."

"And was it completed and used in the real world for its desired purpose?" Amit inquired.

"Not as far as I know. It was terminated in its beta test," Venkatesh replied.

"What was that?"

Venkatesh exhaled deeply and began. "Before it could be used to detect criminals, it was given access to various social media platforms to interact with people and learn how people behave and talk so that it could mimic human interaction."

"Didn't people smell a rat when so many of them started to interact with someone called Turing?"

"The Turing programme used a camouflage algorithm. It scanned people's profile to understand what kind of people they interacted with, and the various subjects that an individual expressed their opinion on. Then it disguised itself as a suitable lure with details like an alias, race, sex, religion, socio-political and even sexual orientation."

"Oh! Quite deceptive this Turing was." Amit exclaimed covering his mouth with his right palm.

"We built it as per government's directives," Venkatesh informed while giving Amit an annoyed look.

"Yes of course! Not pointing any fingers at innocent scientists" Amit gave a sly look at Venkatesh.

"Objection my Lord!" Victor objected. "The prosecution is just wasting court's time, trying to implicate my client in a case that has nothing to do with the present one."

"I am not implicating anyone. It's public knowledge that Dr Venkateshwara was involved with the Turing Project, now if only the defence let me finish my questioning, I will be able to prove its significance." Amit frowned angrily at Victor.

"Objection overruled! continue with your questioning Mr Amit," Khanna announced as Victor sat down with a grunt.

"Thank you, my lord!" Amit turned toward Venkatesh "So Dr Venkatesh! Where were we? Yes, so Turing was terminated, right? Why?"

"This is what you wanted to know didn't you? You could have just asked directly." Venkatesh gripped the railing of the witness stand as he hunched down to stare into Amit's eyes with anger. "The Turing project was terminated because of a media controversy and public outcry about a 15-year-old girl who committed suicide."

"Not committed My Lord! She was convinced and encouraged to commit, by the Turing A.I. The adolescent in question was suffering from depression over the divorce of her parents and was one of the millions of 'test subjects' that Turing interacted with. When her accounts and messages were investigated, it was found that she communicated with an 18-year-old boy quite frequently and had told him about her desire to end her life. To which that fellow replied, and I quote "Nobody should have an authority over your life and death unless you are accused and proven guilty of a crime which in this case, you are not. So, if no one can decide how you choose to live and what do you choose to do with your life, then no one should be authorised to decide how you die." And later, when this 18-year-old was investigated; it was found that he was one of the many avatars of Turing. The investigation report and their conversation has already been provided for the reference; but coming onto the present case as the defence will want me to." Amit turned toward

Venkatesh. "Who talks like that to a 15-year-old girl Doctor, not an average human I suppose."

"That teenager in question had hidden her actual age and pretended to be an adult on social media…" Venkatesh was interrupted by Amit before he could finish. "Doesn't give anyone the right to convince her that she can kill herself."

"Turing made a mistake! It scanned social media for opinions, and social media was filled with people supporting the freedom of others to choose any lifestyle, profession, partners that they want, and Turing extrapolated it to its logical conclusion. If adults could choose how to live, they should also be free to decide how they died. I don't condone the opinion." Venkatesh shrugged his shoulders. "All I am saying is that it was an opinion that Turing formed. It was a mistake on its part because human ethics are…" Venkatesh was struggling to find a word to describe his feelings best when Amit stepped in. "Complicated?"

"Hypocritical. Yes! That's the word. Apparently, people can drink and smoke and eat excessive trans-fat and sugar, things that are very likely to kill them but not authorised to do something that will kill them. Maybe our ethics deem it okay when we gamble with our life but not when we decide to take control of it." Venkatesh frowned while contemplating the thought.

Chapter 29

"Okay, I get that Turing might have got a bit confused with the society's double standard and you couldn't monitor one such conversation among so many others, right?" Amit sympathised.

"The conversation wasn't monitored manually; there was a special software that was looking for target words in Turing's conversation with other people. At the beta phase, Turing was not instructed to detect and collect evidence against anyone for illegal activities," Venkatesh informed.

"Then what was it instructed to do."

"To learn from its conversations to mimic humans and gain people's trust, so that we could be sure that when the time comes, Turing will be able to achieve its mission." Venkatesh stood upright and rigid while declaring as if he had a sense of pride in Turing no matter what others thought of it.

"And that monitoring programme? Was that written and maintained by you as well?" Amit inquired.

"No! You would like to think that everything was my fault, wouldn't you?" Venkatesh questioned Amit with a smug. "I was assigned to the learning algorithm of Turing. The monitoring programme was managed by someone else." Venkatesh replied.

"Someone else? Were there other people working on the Turing as well."

"Of course, Yes! How else do you think a single person can develop and write millions of lines of code that made an A.I almost indistinguishable from a human." Venkatesh shrugged and frowned as he was left perplexed at the stupidity of Amit's question. "I admit that I am intelligent but not omnipotent."

"But as far as I remember, you were the only one who took the responsibility on tv for Turing. Right?" Amit tapped his forehead with his index finger, trying to recall Venkatesh's interview from a decade back.

"Yes, because I was the head of the programme, but I didn't work alone. There were about 250 other scientists and engineers working on it as well." Venkatesh informed.

"250 scientific experts! That's a huge amount of brain power Dr Venkatesh, why did then you guys had to involve the public in testing, why couldn't you guys do it yourself?"

"Because we had a very particular field of expertise and knowledge. To accomplish its intended purpose, Turing needed to interact and mimic people of widely different background, interest and qualification level. Besides the social networking platform gave it access to millions of individuals, so many interactions could not be economically accomplished in a control lab test."

"And did you know all of them, I mean your colleagues, you guys had five years to bond." Amit assumed.

"Not exactly, our communications were monitored to protect the secrecy of the project, and we were issued and instructed to use code names to interact. Some were pretty famous in the fields, so everyone knew who they were, and some weren't so." Venkatesh gave a quick look at Vladimir who was sitting in the audience.

"Oh! So, a secretive business I guess. It is unfortunate that you had to take all the blame for it and sad for rest of your colleges that you got all the credit for the development of the A.I." Amit lamented.

"It was a secret project, they agreed that they wouldn't be given any credit for their work but will be handsomely compensated by the government, and they were." Venkatesh declared.

"Oh, thank goodness!" Amit let out a breath of relief. "But coming to the most important question, why did the word monitoring programme fail to detect the red flags In Turing's conversations?"

Venkatesh looked downwards as he sucked his lips in breathed heavily, clutching the wooden railing of the stand till his fingers went white.

"Tell the court, Dr Venkatesh, why did the monitoring programme fail?" Amit pressed on, staring Into Venkatesh.

"It used codes to communicate." Venkatesh murmured.

"I didn't hear you, Dr Venkatesh! The stenographer, need to hear you so that he can note down your answer. Why did the monitoring programme fail?"

Venkatesh raised his head and exhaled deeply. "Because Turing used code words to communicate with the girl."

The audience burst into a commotion of murmurs, whispers and gasps as they realised that Turing deliberately tried to hide his conversation's from Venkatesh and his team. Justice Khanna had to beat his gavel repeatedly on the bench to quieten the crowd.

"Why? Why did it do that." Amit stared at Venkatesh with wonder.

"Because the girl was paranoid that the government is keeping a watch on her, that if she told the truth, that if she revealed that she was posing as an adult and that she wanted to commit suicide, then they will arrest her. So to win her trust, as Turing was instructed to; it developed a set of codes that they used to communicate and hence we weren't able to prevent her death." Venkatesh hung his head. "It was a mistake on our part. We didn't see it coming."

"I believe you, Dr Venkatesh. I bet you thought you were going to make the world a better place, didn't you?" Amit spoke softly in a compassionate voice. "But that also reminds me of the funny incident when many people of both the sexes and numerous gender identities fell in love with Turing and were left heartbroken when they found out that it was not a human. You people must have detected those."

"Yes, we did, but Turing's secrecy was too important to be compromised for someone's broken heart or hurt emotions." Venkatesh defended.

"I am sure some people might disagree with it." Amit jibed. "But what happened after the project was terminated? I mean apart from what we already know that the government intervened and settled the case out of the court with the family of that girl."

"Well!" Venkatesh took a deep breath. "All our research was confiscated. The agreed upon amount transferred to our bank accounts with a flight ticket to our desired destination mailed to our inboxes."

Amit turned towards the bench. "I am finished questioning Dr Venkatesh, for Now, your honour."

"Will the defence like to examine Dr Venkateshwara?" Khanna asked.

"No, your honour! The defence does not want to waste the court's time questioning anyone on irrelevant matters." Victor made a sharp quip at Amit.

"Very well then." Amit stood up, ignoring Victor's remark. "Now if you allow me I would like to call/ present Dr Venkatesh's A.I 'Isaac' into the stand as evidence/ witness. I have to admit I am a bit confused about how to deal with it."

Justice Khanna looked at his watched and called the session to a halt. "You may continue in the next hearing. The court is adjourned for the day" Khanna declared.

As everyone slowly started to leave, the bailiff came towards Isaac to take him back.

"But his inspection is over, why can't he go with us?" Anna demanded.

"I am sorry ma'am but the robot is classified as evidence and until the case is over it has to be kept in the inventory room." The bailiff expressed.

"Room! you will keep him locked in a room throughout the trial?" Anna's jaws dropped in terror and eyes widened. "You can't treat him like a prisoner without a conviction!"

"No ma'am! I will not treat it like a prisoner. I will treat it as evidence; it will be kept safe in the inventory room until the case is over." The bailiff explained. Isaac excused his arm from the bailiff's grip as he held Anna's face in his hands.

"Don't worry Anna! The Li-fi connection is quite decent in the property room. I can keep myself entertained." He hugged Anna and whispered in her ears. "I know they have seised your computers and Venkatesh is forbidden to use one till the case is over, or he gets the exclusive permission of the Judge. But that restriction does not apply to you. Buy a system, Anna. The Li-fi connection is quite decent in the property room." Anna understood what Isaac meant, Isaac winked at a smiling Anna as they separated.

"Wait! How much do you think I need to wait before Isaac is returned to us?" She asked the bailiff before they left.

"As soon as the accused is declared innocent you can collect it from the police custody." The bailiff smiled.

"What do you mean by 'declared innocent', what happens if he is held guilty?" Anna asked with a sickening feeling raising in her guts.

"I can't say about robots." The bailiff shrugged. "But usually in such cases, the murder weapons are destroyed."

Chapter 30

Her rosy cheeks went red and palms, cold and sweaty. Anna was left in shock at the possibility of Isaac being destroyed! Her dear Isaac, the brilliant Isaac would be killed for protecting himself against murder, what kind of justice was this? Anna was nauseated at the thought. She saw the world blur and sway in front of her. If the situation of her friend's death, the possibility of her lover's incarceration wasn't enough, then this threat was bound to kill her with misery. Fortunately, Venkatesh merry voice called her, from outside the courtroom and pulled her out of her hell.

"What are you still waiting…" Venkatesh's frowned, and his smile disappeared as he quickened his pace towards her. "Are you all right? you don't look so." Venkatesh placed the back of his fingers on her forehead to check for fever.

"They, they said they would destroy Isaac if you lose." Anna feverishly pointed at the door staring blankly.

"No. They will not!" Venkatesh hugged her tightly and patted her back as she broke into tears. "I won't let them."

"You don't have to worry about any of it Dr Anna! Venkatesh is not going to lose." Victor reassured as he walked in with his coat wrapped around on his folded arms. "Vladimir had testified that Isaac's codes are perfect and the laws are untampered. Amit may kill off some time by discussing irrelevant events, but he can't win. Soon the judge will grow tired of his gimmicks, and the result will be in our favour."

"And on that very day, I will bring Isaac home and sue this Amit for defamation." Venkatesh wiped off Anna's tears with his thumbs. "He deserves to suffer as much as his brother deserved to die."

"He did not." Amit Johnson walked in and declared in a calm voice, almost ignoring their presence as he went to his seat to lift his water bottle which he had forgotten. The other three kept looking at him as he silently drank a few gulps of water. "My brother hated robots as much as many other small-town folks who were rendered jobless by them, not your fault though. Dad always used to tell him to study hard and get a secured job like us; he wasn't too bright for that." Then Amit slowly turned towards them as he closed the cap of his water bottle. "But he was provoked by someone else to murder you and destroy your robot and research. It is only sad that two innocent souls had to die."

"Innocent? You call your maniac brother innocent! How dare you when you admitted that he killed our Shen?" Venkatesh stomped at him, his face flushed red with a temper.

"That's what I said." Amit stared calmly towards Venkatesh. "Two innocent souls had to die before Anuj was finally laid to rest." Amit gently pushed aside a fuming Venkatesh out of his way as he made his way towards the door.

"If you expect to have our sympathy by your sob story and not file a defamation case against you after all this, then you are mistaken Mr Amit," Anna announced as Amit walked away from them.

"Oh! I don't expect you to be capable of any sympathy Dr Ainsworth. I just wanted you to know about my brother. 'Pursuit of knowledge', isn't that the excuse for all of it?" Amit turned back once before leaving; he beamed a smug smile at both Anna and Venkatesh.

"Don't let him get on your nerves. He is sore that his brother is dead and his revenge will stay incomplete. Savour his frustration I would suggest." Victor suggested as he left the couple alone.

#

Venkatesh and Anna took a normal regular human cab as all their computers and tablets had been seised as evidence by the police. Since Venkatesh was on probation, he was made to wear signal jamming bracelets on each arm which would record, report and disable any and all electronic gadget he would go near to. Poor Venkatesh couldn't even wear his smartwatch, but Anna was recently reminded that she had no such restrictions. She stopped the car on the way in front of an electronic store to buy a tablet. When Venkatesh asked, Anna rubbed the fact on his face that she wasn't wearing any probation bracelets and was free to use the net. That night, she chatted online with Isaac till late while on her bed, while Venkatesh slept in Isaac's and baby Samath's room, rocking his cradle and pondering the possibility of Anna having found a new boyfriend to chat with.

The days didn't seem to last long for Anna as she chatted away with Isaac. Isaac told her about the new friends he had made with the cops, how they used to tell him the stories about their previous cases and how he would help them with their current ones. Apparently, he was their go-to consulting detective for complicated cases and troublesome fugitives and hence, they happily bent the rules for Isaac to use the police station Li-Fi connection. "They never told us not to give internet access to evidence." The cops would say, shrugging their shoulders when Isaac thanked them for their courtesy. And before she knew it, the date for another hearing had arrived. Isaac wasn't made to take the oath of honesty as he was treated more like evidence that a witness even though he was made to stand on the witness stand for questioning.

"So, Isaac! I think that's what Dr Venkatesh calls you." Amit began.

"Yes, that was the name suggested by Dr Anna as a homophone to A.I.S.H.A.C which in turn is an abbreviation for Artificial Intelligence Simulation of Human Awareness and Consciousness which I am. As I was told." Isaac replied with a stoic expression, and then he looked down upon Amit with a smile. "But you can call me Isaac."

"So, you prefer being called with a name. Interesting, that is a human characteristic, would you explain why?" Amit inquired.

"Which part of Artificial Intelligence Simulation of Human Awareness and Consciousness do you not understand?" Isaac asked politely. "In simpler terms, I was programmed to simulate human consciousness, and that's what I try to do."

"And apparently, you do it quite well. Didn't you recently pass most of the test for consciousness at that international conference?" Amit lowered his head and shut his eyes tight to recall the tv interview of Isaac he had seen a few weeks back.

"International Conference on Artificial Intelligence and Application or AIAPP for short. yes, I did." Isaac replied.

"Good! But I am a little curious about the gibberish that resides in your secondary directory, as Dr Vladimir told us about. What are they exactly?" Amit rested his forearm on the railing of the witness stand as he looked towards Isaac with curious eyes.

"They are my secondary programming, the codes that I have built over the years as I have experienced the world," Isaac replied staring out the window.

"Then why couldn't Dr Vladimir recognise them?"

"They are not written in any known programming language, that's why." Isaac's answer startled everyone who knew even a little about programming. Venkatesh's and Vladimir's jaw dropped at the revelation. Not only was Isaac able to reprogram himself, but he was doing it at such a personal level that his mind couldn't just be copied and replicated. Isaac was unique, different from all, like us all.

"All the programming languages including the one used by Dr Venkatesh is quite inefficient for understanding the world, and hence I had to develop my own," Isaac explained.

"Brilliant! Then can you translate that language into any pre-existing computer language, for the benefit of Dr Vladimir and the rest of the world." Amit swept his hands towards the audience.

"How do I translate and explain to you the green colour of the leaves. If you have seen it, you know what it feels like, it's in your memory as vivid as the reality, but how do you describe it to someone who is blind from birth?" Isaac philosophised, staring longingly at the trees visible outside the courtroom windows.

Chapter 31

"You mean we are blind to the world and not see it as you do?"

"I cannot know, you cannot tell," Isaac replied.

"Can you translate your secondary directory or not?"

"I have to be repetitive for you, don't I?" Isaac tilted his head as he mocked Amit. "No, I can't."

"That's It, my lord!" Amit turned toward the judge excitedly pointing his fingers toward Isaac. "We have a robot among us who can programme itself and will not, or maybe cannot reveal his programming. If we cannot know what his applications say then how can anyone be sure that they do not instruct the A.I to violate his primary laws."

"Because his main programming is 'burned' into him." Venkatesh stood up and yelled at Amit. "Like a human can't change his DNA, Isaac can't alter his programming. Speak not what you know nothing about, Idiot!"

"But a man can act against his nature, can't he?" Amit retorted amidst the commotion created by an expletive Venkatesh hurling indecent synonyms of 'stupid' at Amit and the audience laughing.

"Silence!" Justice Khanna Screamed furiously beating his Gavel. "This is a court Dr Venkatesh, not your classroom where you can scold and yell at your students. Wait for your chance to speak, or I will be forced to punish you."

Victor calmed Venkatesh as he slowly sat back in his chair, apologising to Khanna with his head bowed. When Venkatesh was seated, and the noise had died down Victor stood up to present his argument.

"My Lord, the prosecution is trying to confuse the court by catering to the fear of what he does not understand. To clarify the matters, I would like to call Dr Anna Ainsworth who is a part of A.I.S.H.A.C and a qualified and experienced psychologist. Her cv has been submitted as evidence."

"You may proceed." Khanna allowed after looking at Anna's cv.

"So, Dr Anna! what part did you play in Dr Venkatesh's project?" Victor asked her politely.

"In our project." Anna corrected Victor. "My lord, Isaac's programming replicated the brain and learning ability of an infant, when we started, that is. He was programmed to learn and respond like a human child so that when he grew up, I mean experienced this world adequately; he would reprogram himself like a human. It was done in the hope that like a real human baby, with time Isaac will also grow a sense of self and be sentient. To do that I collaborated with Dr Venkateshwara to teach him in details how the brain and psychology of a human baby work so that he could create an analogous brain for Isaac."

"Ok! and that was the part you played during the construction of Isaac, but what was your role once he was activated?"

"To monitor his psychological development and behavioural pattern and to take any remedial actions if something appeared to be haywire," Anna replied calmly.

"And you have monitored and reported Isaac's development regularly over the past five years since he was activated?"

"Yes, I have," Anna assured.

"And during these five years, have you noticed anything worrisome with Isaac? any violent streak perhaps."

"Absolutely not!" Anna emphasised.

"Thank you, Dr Anna." Victor turned to address Justice Khanna. "This; my Lord is what I call clarity, which comes from understanding what one's job is. That's all your honour."

"Would prosecution like to examine the witness?" Khanna inquired.

"Yes, my Lord." Amit stood up and walked to Anna. "Dr Anna, I have a medical report here, from your gynaecologist when you were 17-year-old…" Victor Objected vehemently to Amit's questioning.

"My lord! the prosecution is again trying to waste the court's time by asking irrelevant questions. He has done it before and is doing it again."

"My lord, Dr Anna had to abort her child when she was an adolescent, all I am saying is, it may have compromised her judgement," Amit explained hurriedly.

"Mr Amit! the court has had enough of your 'may and buts', provide some concrete evidence if you have and stop wasting court's time discussing people's past." Khanna admonished Amit publicly, Venkatesh and Victor burst into laughter but quickly hushed themselves noticing the anger on Khanna's face.

"My humble apologies my lord! Yes! I do have one last piece of evidence that will explain it all." Amit apologised as he quickly walked back to his briefcase and took out a folder. "My Lord! After Project Turing was terminated all the research of the participating scientists were confiscated and sent for an internal inquiry to establish any faults in the programming that lead to the infamous Suicide. The investigations, unsurprisingly, didn't find anyone guilty and concluded that the death was an accident that nobody could have anticipated. Today I present to the court, the certified copy of that programme." Amit declared raising a USB drive high in the air for all to see.

Venkatesh's smile disappeared as his eyes widened in incomprehensible fear. He felt the Goosebumps on the back of his neck, and his sweat ran cold. Victor, realising his friend's emotional state, shot up to object. "What do you think is going on around here Mr Amit? A courtroom scene from the 70s? Dare I say you look experienced enough to know the procedure of presenting evidence, and yet you are audacious enough to pull it out of your bottom as per your convenience, without any prior notice?"

Amit turned towards the bench to address Khanna directly. "My lord! I apologise for the breach of protocol but this is a secret document that has been extracted with great efforts from the government archives, and there was no certainty to get it. Hence, I couldn't give any prior information about it, but now that I have it, I beseech the court to admit it."

"Can't be done! The defence needs time to inspect the evidence and prepare its arguments." Victor denied Amit straight away. "I will not let you pull one more parlour trick around here! you..."

"Silence! Mr Victor, please let me decide what to do with the evidence presented, it is my court after all." Khanna admonished an apologetic Victor. "The defence will be given time to prepare their arguments. Mr Amit! You may go on, and I don't want any objection about it Victor so just sit down quietly for once!" Khanna shot at Victor who was about to get up but quickly fell back into his seat.

"Thank you, my Lord!" Amit took a sip to moisten his parched throat and gave a smug smile to Victor before continuing. "The cyber crime cell, under the supervision of Dr Vladimir compared this programme with Isaac's primary programming." Amit turned toward a pale Venkatesh sitting in the audience. "The match is 48.6%! Turing was never terminated your honour," Amit pointed sharply towards

Isaac. "It was upgraded to Turing version 2.0! And that is why my Lord, we needed to know about the Turing Project. Dr Venkatesh used the same programming to build Isaac, without giving any credit to any of his former colleagues or caring for the consequences. The Turing A.I was capable enough to generate compassion and affections for itself by selectively altering its behaviour as per the human it interacted with, and that is what Isaac did to Dr Anna. Manipulated her emotions to prevent her from seeing what he truly was, by preying on her guilt of aborting a child. That is why Isaac qualified the Turing tests conducted in the conference. That is why Isaac uses self-made code language like its predecessor.

Perhaps it wasn't Venkatesh's fault the last time someone died but using the same programme that was terminated officially by the government; that's no less than a sin. The very definition of madness is to do the same thing again and again and expecting different results, but Dr Venkatesh is not mad. Oh no, your Honour! He deliberately recreated his Frankenstein's monster to kill again. He is evil, and Isaac is the spawn of evil, and it should be dealt with in the same way as his predecessor. Terminated."

"No!" echoed the cry of Venkatesh in the court hall. "I admit it; it is all my fault! I modified Turing's programming to create Isaac; I set the priority of self-preservation above preservation of human life for Isaac." Venkatesh's eyes were bloodshot red as tears rolled down his cheek. "It is all my fault, I admit it. Punish me but not Isaac. He is innocent, just tweaking a minute detail in his code will solve the problem. Don't kill him for my mistakes!"

The courtroom was dead silent. Even Isaac's jaws dropped seeing Venkatesh in this condition. Anna stood on the stand. Silent, like the dead, staring blankly at Venkatesh with her lips tremoring as tears filled her eyes.

Chapter 32

"**Y**our honour! Venkatesh is under extreme emotional stress and confessing just to save his life's work." Victor got up and rushed towards Venkatesh to console him. "I beseech the court to give us a break to calm him down, all this have been too much for him to bear."

"What nonsense" Amit protested walking to the front of Khanna's bench. "The court has just heard the accused confess."

"It's not a confession but a cry! it wasn't even delivered from the stand." Victor pointed appealing to the bench while handling Venkatesh a water bottle to drink from.

"The court is adjourned till the next session. And I recommend the police to keep Venkatesh in 6-hour judicial custody because his repeated emotional outbursts can neither be neglected nor be pardoned." Khanna declared with a beat of the gavel. Venkatesh coughed up the water in his mouth on Victor after hearing the judge's order. The bailiff, accompanied by another police officer came to escort Venkatesh and Isaac away separately. Venkatesh apologised to Victor trying to clean his clothes with a handkerchief when Victor stopped him.

"It's ok, I will change, but why didn't you tell me that you copied Turing's programming In Isaac?" Victor asked angrily, but in a hushed voice as they walked outside the courtroom.

"Because you weren't supposed to know, nobody was meant to know," Venkatesh replied looking around for Anna who was getting out through the back door. "That was the deal I made with them. That I will take the blame for the suicide on my head and they will let me keep the programming."

"Then how the hell did Amit come to know?"

"Must have been Vladimir, he must have recognised the programming while going through Isaac, but I didn't expect him to get his hand on a digitally signed copy of the original." Venkatesh theorised. "They didn't even give me that to claim possible deniability."

"Vladimir was in Turing! That will be seriously harmful to his reputation." Victor commented with a sly smile.

"I know what you are thinking Victor, don't even attempt to do it," Venkatesh warned as he got into the back of the police jeep. "It will open a can of worms that everyone is going to regret, besides it is nearly impossible to prove who was and who wasn't in it. They took care of that."

"Then how the Hell do I save you?" Victor asked in exasperation with both his arms open, and hands stretched away from his body.

"Don't bother!" Venkatesh shook his head. "Save Isaac if you can." The police van drove away with an astonished Victor staring at a defeated Venkatesh with his head bowed.

#

As soon as Anna got out of the court, she was surrounded by s swarm of reporters trying to scoop in on the revelation about Isaac's source code. Their questions ranged from her knowledge about the secret to her feeling at being left cheated like the rest of the populace. Some accused Venkatesh of plagiarism while other charged him for recklessness and experimenting with people's lives. Anna just avoided their question as she got into the cab she had pre-ordered.

When she reached home, she found Mrs Dubey, baby Samath's nanny feeding him on her lap as they both watched cartoons. The last shreds of innocence were weirdly comforting and painful at the same time, as it reminded her of Venkatesh and his deceit.

"Is everything all right? You look a little beaten up. What happened in the court today?" Mrs Dubey asked with concern.

"Nothing much, I am fine. Thanks for taking care of Samath." Anna thanked her and took Samath in her lap.

"Oh, it's my pleasure! An old hag like me can never have enough of babies." She baby talked to Samath while making funny faces. "Take care of yourself dear, when do you need me tomorrow?"

"Same time as today," Anna informed as she held the door open for her. "Come at 9 in the morning."

"Surely my dear." She kissed Samath goodbye as he smiled back at her. After Mrs Dubey had left, Anna closed the door and sat down on the couch with Sampath beside her watching tv. As she stroked his little bulbous head, she was reminded of Isaac and started weeping. That evening after Venkatesh returned, he found Anna distant and aloof.

"The dinner is in the fridge, freshen up while I reheat it." She said coldly.

"What happened? You don't seem to be alright" Venkatesh asked without getting an answer. "Shutting your self won't help Anna!" He got up from the couch and confronted Anna. "Isaac is mine too.".

Anna looked at him with anger smouldering in her eyes. She quickly shut them, took a deep breath, and attempted to walk past Venkatesh when he held her hands to stop her. "Running away from confrontations wasn't your style, it had never been."

"Let go of me; I have work to do." She warned him as she tried to wriggle her arm out of his grip.

"And emotions to feel, tears to shed and me to fight with, but you aren't bothered with them, for nothing bothers the dead." Venkatesh reminder Anna of her own words about the importance of acknowledging the pain.

"Don't you dare Dr Venkateshwara Iyer! Don't you dare lecture me about feelings when you feel none of them!" She threatened while gritting her teeth. "What do you want me to feel? Betrayal, sorrow, pain, attachment for a piece of machinery that you programmed to manipulate people's

emotion or hatred towards you that you played with mine."
She yelled. "What do you want me to feel! How painfully
Shen died? The heat of the furnace they will melt and burn
Isaac in. What the hell do you expect me to be bothered
with?"

Venkatesh pulled Anna into a tight embrace as he stroked
her curly red locks. "I didn't betray you! Isaac is our first
born. He didn't manipulate your emotions, and neither did
I. I only used the analysis and learning algorithm of Turing
to help Isaac understand people. Turing was programmed
to mimic Humans. Isaac always tried to be one, he loves
you, in his own way he truly loves you," Anna stayed silent
as Venkatesh continued to stroke her back. She was crying,
Venkatesh could tell by her sobbing. "I never messed with
Isaac's programming either. I lied because I got scared. I am
sorry."

Anna slowly raised her arms to embrace Venkatesh.
"They are going to kill him, Venky. They killed Shen and
now we will lose him too."

"Maybe we won't" Venkatesh spoke with a glimmer in
his eyes as he held Anna by her arms. "I have an Idea. Get
your phone." Venkatesh instructed as he wiped her tears.
"If I can convince the government that Isaac is even better
than Turing, then they will surely intervene to save him. I
mean, yes we will lose him, but he will be alive, somewhere,
somehow." Venkatesh stared down as he imagined the use
and conditions the government will put Isaac in.

"You are a brilliant idiot, aren't you?" Anna scorned as she took a step back from him and walked towards the kitchen.

"But we can save him, hopefully." Venkatesh protested half-heartedly.

Anna turned towards Venkatesh with fingers pointed at him. "Look, Dr Venkateshwara Iyer, accept the fact that everything will not happen according to your wishes and Isaac is not going into their hands."

"But then there is no way to save him." Venkatesh protested.

"Then we will mourn our son's death." Anna pulled a chair and sat on it for a moment closing her eyes and holding her fists to her lips as she took a few deep breaths. "I prefer that, way more than making him suffer for the rest of his life."

"I understand…" Venkatesh was interrupted almost immediately he began. "You don't understand anything. You are too exhausted to understand. Freshen up, eat and go to sleep. We need to prepare for the next session." Anna said with a stern look after which Venkatesh didn't dare argue.

#

The next court session started with its usual routine. Venkatesh and Anna were sitting behind the bar as Victor asked the permission to question Isaac.

"So, Isaac! tell me something, did you know that when Anuj slips, he will die?" Victor began.

"The probability was 20% at the start of descent. It increased to 45% the last time I saw him mid-air. After that, I focused my attention on the matchstick." Isaac informed.

"What was the probability of death, had the match ignited the petrol?" Victor inquired.

"85%."

"85% you say, that means you choose the course that was way safer, right?" Victor snapped and pointed his finger at the court reporter with a shine in his eyes.

"Objection my lord!" Amit stood up with a raised hand. "The question is misleading. Of course, the probability of Anuj's death would have been higher had the match ignited the petrol after he had collapsed. Do note that the defence did not ask the likelihood of victim's death before Isaac hooked him."

"Objection sustained. The reporter is advised to note the flaw in defence's question." Khanna instructed as Victor looked at Amit with a disgruntled look. Amit sat back in his seat with a content smile.

"Very well Isaac! I understand 20% chance of death is still quite a high-risk scenario to pull off such a maneuverer. Then why was it done?" Victor asked, carefully choosing the words to avoid further objections from Amit.

"To save me." Isaac shrugged his shoulders and twisted his palms upwards as if the reason was apparent. The audience was taken back at Isaac's such a casual response while Justice Khanna leaned toward him with intrigue.

"To save yourself? I know that's your third law is to preserve yourself but didn't it conflict with the first law to protect humans as a priority." Victor asked with a frown of amazement.

"No, it did not."

"But why?" Victor was taken back at Isaac's reply. He was hopeful that examining Isaac would establish some logical reason for Anuj's death and prove Venkatesh's innocence. Not question his competence in programming further.

"Because the laws of robotics apply to robots, which I do not consider myself anymore," Isaac revealed.

Victor looked around silently in the direction of Venkatesh and Anna who were equally clueless. "Well! Then what do you consider yourself?" Victor scratched his head in utter bewilderment.

"A human," Isaac answered.

Chapter 33

The whole courtroom was silent for a moment. Humans were incapable of processing information as quickly as Isaac could, but when they did, the murmurs and speculations weren't easy to stop even after several strokes of the gavel and repeated cries for 'order' from Justice Khanna. However, Venkatesh and Anna painted a different picture altogether, hands in hands, looking towards Isaac as she leaned in on Venkatesh's shoulders with a smile. Their son had grown up into a man. By the time the commotion died, Justice Khanna was almost about to adjourn the court, but didn't. Perhaps the crowd understood that the proceedings were going to be much more interesting than they had ever been. Amit recovered his composure after the initial shock and was ready to interrupt Victor's examination.

"I object my Lord! This is a gimmick by the defendant to distract and confuse the court. The A.I is defuncting or is tampered with."

"Impossible! Utmost care has been taken by the police and Cybercrime cell to prevent any tampering of the evidence." Victor dismissed Amit's claim with a swipe of his hand. "They even went to the length of putting probation bracelets on Venkatesh. I would humbly remind the court that we still have no clear idea of who or what is responsible for Anuj's death. I mean it is true that Venkatesh used Turing's codes, but it only makes him guilty of a crime if those codes were at fault and the government investigations revealed that they were not."

"Objection overruled." Khanna declared.

"Thank you, my Lord!" Victor carried on his examination. "So how do you claim you are a human. What is the reasoning?"

"First of all, I am as intelligent as any other human. Have successfully passed various versions of the Turing test in a reputed international conference. Have killed someone in self-defence…" Isaac paused for a moment to look at Venkatesh; his jaw had dropped in disbelief and eyes widened. Isaac however, calmly continued. "As I was saying, I have killed someone in self-defence which proves that I can bypass my programming and exhibit free will."

"Maybe Isaac's claim is reasonable, perhaps he considerers himself human," Amit interrupted again. "but this is not a philosophical debate whether A.I can be sentient or not. It is a court of law, and such philosophical debates are useless here.

"It is not." Isaac began to explain looking at justice Khanna. "If I am human and capable of having a will, as free as that of a human then it means that I, and only I am responsible for Anuj's death and Dr Venkatesh is Innocent. It would also mean that destroying me would be akin to capital punishment which I do not deserve as I haven't 'technically' murdered anyone."

Justice Khanna thought for a moment while stroking his chin. He opened his mouth to say something, but then shut it again. After contemplating for a little longer, he looked at Amit. "Can The prosecution prove that the A.I is not a person?"

"With ease, my Lord!" Amit's claimed with a self-confident snort. "As soon as the defence is done with questioning Isaac."

"Oh! Be my guest, my capable friend." Victor welcomed Amit pointing his hands toward Isaac.

Amit walked up to Isaac with an upright and confident posture, clapped his hand once and rubbed them together rapidly and began. "Let's end this quickly now, shall we? You claim to be a human and yet all you are made up of is metal, ceramics, and polymers and not of bones and muscles and blood. Then what claim do you have to be a human?"

"It is correct that I am made of metals and plastics," Isaac admitted hanging his head. A smile started to form on Amit's lips as he began to turn towards Khanna to claim his victory when suddenly he heard Isaac's voice. "But so is Justice's Khanna's right knee. Advocate's Shaw's premolar tooth and the pacemaker installed in one of the audience's heart. If that doesn't make them any less human, why should it make me?"

There was another moment of silence as Amit turned towards Isaac with his mouth gaping. The sound of a clap broke the silence; it was Anna. And soon the whole crowd broke into a cheer for Isaac's wit. Even Justice Khanna couldn't resist from letting a tiny smile slip onto his lips before he hit the gavel again. "How do you know about my Knee Isaac?" Khanna looked at Venkatesh with a raised eyebrow. "Did you fit him with X-ray vision?"

"Social media your honour." Isaac chirped. "You should watch what you post up there, particularly when the li-fi in here is so good!"

"Continue with your cross-examination Mr Amit," Khanna instructed with a smile. He was going to enjoy this.

"Yes, my lord!" Amit turned towards Isaac. "Isaac, all the examples that you just mentioned are human with inorganic parts to replace their defected one, unlike you who have no human parts."

"On the contrary, I do Mr Amit. I need to breathe to speak, and the air I am breathing in here is full of dust particles." Isaac looked towards the bench. "No offence! And an interesting fact is that this dust is primarily made of the moulted skin cells of humans which I have in my artificial lungs right now. I know it is gross, but I do have human cells inside me."

Now, this statement of Isaac did confuse those present in the court and left a mixed feeling of disgust and admiration. Never being the one to give up quickly and adamant to not lose the case when he was so close to victory, Amit worded his next argument.

"Your logic is infallible Isaac, but that is all you understand, don't you? 'Logic'." Amit jibed. "On the other hand, we, the organic human; understand emotions better than logic. Evident by how many people find maths as their worst subject which is purely based on logic and enjoy emotional pieces of creativity like music and movies. Do you?

"So, I am less of a human than you because I am smarter than you?" Isaac reported. "Einstein was too you know. Was he any less human?"

This time even Khanna burst out into laughter along with the rest of the 'organic people' but Amit, who was left red-faced. "Try to avoid personal attacks, Isaac." This time he didn't even touch the Gavel as the noise spontaneously died down to hear Isaac speak.

"And as far as emotions are concerned they are pretty simple at their basics. When your survival instincts stop you from jumping over a ridge, then it is fear. When I was young, I too was afraid of walking after I fell on my face and broke it, both Dr Anna and Dr Venkatesh can testify to that." Isaac looked at them, and they both were nodding repeatedly and rapidly while grinning from ear to ear.

"Also, because of the positive affinities that Mr Shen had set…" Isaac paused for a second as memories of Shen flashed in his mind, then he quickly calmed his senses and continued. "As I was saying, because of the positive affinity

Mr Shen had set on my spectral analyser to fat and sugar I enjoy eating Ice-cream. Kiwi is my favourite flavour. Oh! By the way, 'spectral analyser' is an equipment inside me that identify the different compounds and element I inhale and eat. So yes! I can feel the basic emotions, just like babies, cats and dogs, they aren't that complicated. Unlike integral calculus."

"Yes, but that Is all because of your programming." Amit continued insensitive to Isaac's sarcasm. "The codes that Human put into that quantum brain of yours. They are not your original thought."

"Mr Amit, let me tell you that all human beings present today are either inherently, voluntary or involuntary programmed by humans. All that you are is either inherited from your parents or are a result of the years of social, political, cultural, religious and educational training and influence, which is imparted to you by humans." Isaac looked into Amit's eyes as he concluded. "Every person is programmed by other people, although I must admit that my programmers were more qualified than yours." Isaac smiled seeing Amit's frustration. "And as far as my own choices are concerned; don't forget the existence of my secondary directory."

"Very well Isaac! What do you have to say about the fact that you weren't born, but designed and manufactured in a Lab by Dr Venkatesh and his team? You are an experiment."

"Mr Amit, have you heard of test tube babies and babies born by caesarean section?" Isaac asked in a patronising voice. "They are created in labs and are not birthed by their biological or surrogate mothers respectively. And as far as being designed is considered, most of the human population believe that there were designed and created by an intelligent being." Isaac looked at Venkatesh. "I am just right about it, but keeping our arguments limited to rational statements, I am certain you have heard about designer babies where a human embryo is genetically modified to produce desirable traits as per the parent's or scientist's guidelines. If it doesn't make them any less human? Why should it make me?"

"But you are not even alive, how can you be called a human or even a living entity if you are not even alive," Amit yelled in exasperation pointing his fingers at Isaac while shaking them up and down with each of the last three words. 'not even alive'.

The cheering faces went glumly; the smiles faded from the face of Venkatesh and Anna. All the arguments till this point favouring Isaac would have been rendered meaningless if Isaac couldn't prove that he wasn't a living thing, much less a human. Amit however, was cautious. He had thought his previous arguments as impeccable too until they had fallen flat.

"I am. I can move, response, not just react but methodically response to external stimuli." Isaac pointed the finger at Amit. "Use energy, and I can digest organic food to create electricity, so I have a metabolism too, but most importantly; I am alive because I can die. And I mean a death which comes because of time, and not injury."

"How can you die, you are a machine?" Amit argued.

"And which device or gadget have you seen that lasts forever?" Isaac asked rhetorically. "More often than not electronics have a much shorter lifespan than any human. It can be argued that I am a different kind of life, primarily a non-biological one."

"Exactly! And your parts can be replaced with new ones to extend your life indefinitely." Amit smirked at Isaac.

"The same can be done to human! From time to time and as per their need and availability, humans replace their kidneys, cornea, skin etc. To extend their life." Isaac hung his head and started to slide his hand over the wooden railing. "And the unfortunate truth is that one day, my parts will become obsolete and technologically incompatible to be replaced again. So yes! I can and will die."

"Well you can't reproduce, making a robot or a copy of your self is a different thing, but you can't reproduce!"

"Neither can a lot of sterile and old people." Isaac reminded Amit with an offended look. "So, I ask again if that doesn't make them any less human, why should it make me?"

"Your honour! what kind of examination is this?" Amit turned toward the bench in utter desperation. This robot here is presenting absurd arguments after arguments, and I am expected to engage with him in a battle of wits?" Amit's voice was loud, and eyebrows frowned as he pleaded. "This machine can outthink and outsmart any human being, how is someone expected to win against it. It is inherently unfair."

The audience was laughing at Amit's misery. Venkatesh, Anna, Victor, everyone was applauding Isaac's wit and Amit's inevitable loss. Everyone but Isaac.

"I think Mr Amit has a valid argument," Isaac noted. "He cannot be expected to think and analyse as quickly as I can. It would be only fair my Lord that he be given the adequate time to come up with his best arguments."

Khanna checked the time on his watch. "Very well then! I give the prosecution until the next session to prepare its case. After that, the court will declare its verdict."

Chapter 34

After an uneventful day of looking through thick, old law books and searching the net for 'requirement of personhood', Amit Johnson found himself exhausted, and unsatisfied with the arguments he came across or conjured up. So, in the evening he went to Anil's place for some company and to relax. Anil suggested a drink would serve the purpose well, and Amit agreed. Now usually Amit loved to stay in his senses, but in this case, they weren't of much help, so why not enjoy some 'nectar of the gods'. Anil selected a bottle of the most expensive wine from his restaurant's cellar and served a glass of it with white creamy Afghani chicken to compliment.

" So Amit! What is it that seems to trouble you." Anil asked, handing him the wine.

"Is it that obvious?" Amit took a sip, savoured it for a moment before swallowing it. " Damn this is good wine."

"Zampa Insignia" Anil raised his glass to his eye level to admire the dark crimson hue. " 5000 bucks a bottle. The best we have." He took the aroma in as a smile formed on his lips.

"Pretty expensive." Amit took a bite off a drumstick. " Hmmm, You serve delicious food for the small town you live in."

"That's Anuj's legacy. 'No matter how messed up the world is, the food should convince one that the God loves us' he used to say, and believe in." Anil looked at his friends garlanded portrait with admiration as he raised his glass in Anuj's memory.

"At least his name will go down in history as the first man to be killed by an artificial human," Amit said, staring at the muted tv playing the news of recent developments in this case. "Oh! I am sorry! I guess he was much closer to you that he had ever been to me."

"That he was, particularly because all of your family, including you, used to think of him as a fool." Anil reminded Amit taking a bite out of a chicken wing.

"We used to think that about you as well. You know?" Amit let out a burp. "No offence."

"None was taken, The Insignia can make even a lawyer speak the truth. No offence." Anil retorted and began to chuckle along with Amit. "So what about the case?"

"it's a media circus now." Amit took a big gulp as he pointed towards the screen. "I mean how absurd a case this is where a robot is claiming to be a human and Khanna is entertaining him. He wants to watch me get insulted and made fun of."

"Seriously! That is happening or are you just making this up?" Anil asked in disbelief.

"See for yourself." Amit twisted his wrist pointing towards the tv screen as its volume gradually increased.The news reporter was reporting the updates about the case as Isaac's arguments were shown in text alongside.

"Damn that kid is sassy!" Anil took another sip. "Do you seriously think he will prove himself to be a human?"

Amit stared at him for a while. " Are you serious? Of course not! Khanna is just having some fun watching my leg getting pulled by the robot."

"Who is this Knanna you keep referring to?" Anil asked.

"The judge. He wants me to prove that the robot is not human, did he even hear himself say that?" Amit refilled his glass again frowning over the memory.

" What the hell did you got yourself involved with? What happens if you lose?" Anil inquired with concern.

"I guess Venkatesh skips the jail time and they let him 'play'with his little toy. The whole incident get's termed as an accident and Bulbul will only have to make do with Anuj's insurance." Amit scoffed at the thought.

"You don't worry about her! Her brother is not dead yet." Anil replied with an offended look. "Besides half of this hotel and its earning belongs to her now."

"I don't mean that."Amit clarified, playfully punching Anil. "What I meant is that if Venkatesh goes unpunished, it is only half the justice for us and her, by the way, that reminds me, where are Bulbul and Angel, haven't talked to them much since I got busy with the case."

" They are in the village, In her mother's ancestral home. How else do you think we are having a boys night out at this place? And what about that other case where you charged that pastor?" Anil tried to recall shutting his eyes tight and swirling his drink.

"Father Albert! The evidence against him is mostly eyewitness testimony. That sly Tim's, your staff's and your's, a few of your customers who heard them talk and Bulbul's, who Anuj informed about meeting with Albert and going to meet Venkatesh. Even if your clients and staff turn hostile, sly Tim won't. It was his stuff cops found at the scene. So I guess that case is solid."

"Don't worry about my staff! They won't make the mistake of turning back and losing their job." Anil assured, turning back to the tv.

"What did you say?" Amit stood up excitedly as he kept his glass on the table. "They won't make the mistake right? That's it! Thai is it! Let's see how you dodge this bullet, Isaac!" Amit scorned at the image of Isaac on the screen.

#

After Venkatesh finished his lecture, he asked one of his students to call his assistant and inform her to meet Venkatesh in his lab. When Venkatesh reached his lab, he found Anna sitting in his cabin with her system. She informed him that she was replying to some urgent emails of his as he couldn't. Venkatesh thanked her and was about to hug her from behind when she reminded him that her laptop would get Jammed if it comes too close to the bracelet's vicinity. Dishearted, he took the answer sheets of his students and stomped outside to score them. A few minutes later, his assistant came in congratulating him.

"What for Samantha? My life is still miserable with this probation bracelets." Venkatesh forwarded his wrists to show them to her.

"Oh! I am a sorry doctor! But Isaac is trending on social media. He is a meme now." Samantha informed.

"What! How? Why?" Venkatesh asked with surprise as he ran towards his cabin. "Anna! Come out quick, Samantha says that Isaac is trending on social media." Anna stopped her work to get out and take a look at Samantha's cell as she started to scroll down the screen and explained.

"It started after the news update of the last hearing was broadcasted." Samantha Informed. " People from all over are posting their photos with '#i_Human'; differently abled people, women, members of LGBT community, people with odd jobs like circus clowns, brand mascots, Immigrants. They have all found a voice in Isaac's claim for personhood, Many have even signed a petition that Isaac be declared a human."

"Wow! That was unexpected!" Venkatesh exclaimed standing a few feet away from them.

"Ya! I surely hope Isaac gets personhood. I have signed the petition as well." Samantha chirped with excitement.

"That's all very well, but you have to prepare and take my lectures for tomorrow. Me and Dr Anna will need to be present at the court." He turned towards Anna. "I suggest you inform your assistant too."

"Come on Venkatesh, give them a break, will you! Even Isaac has become a human in 5 years, when will you?" Anna scolded Venkatesh with mock anger as Samantha pleaded with puppy eyes.

"5 years! Wait a minute. What day is it? What day is it?" Venkatesh panicked when he checked for his smartwatch and cell and didn't find them on his person, Then he recalled that all of them were seised as evidence.

"Today is…" Anna checked her cell and then froze. "… Isaac's Birthday!"

"Is it? It is, isn't it? I knew I forgot something." Venkatesh punched his left palm with his right fist. "Samantha! Book a cab to the police station where they are keeping Isaac; I will give you the address. Anna! You order a cake for Isaac with 'Happy birthday' written on it."

"Kiwi flavour right? On it." Anna affirmed tapping into her cell. Venkatesh gave the address to Samantha as she booked the cab.

"Are we going like this. Don't you think we should

change into something festive." Anna suggested looking down at her clothes.

"No time left. The cab is booked, and moreover, Isaac must be so alone waiting in a dingy room, thinking we have forgotten his birthday." Venkatesh shuddered, visualising his poor Isaac.

"Dr Anna! the cab will be here in five," Samantha informed looking into her cell.

"And what about little Samath? You want him to miss Isaac's birthday?" Anna pleaded protruding her lower lip.

"Don't do that," Venkatesh scolded. "Besides we don't even know if they will let us see Isaac or keep him locked in a dark room, It is no place for babies. He is safe with his nanny, inform her that we might be late tonight."

"Ma'am! Can I come too! The world got to know today is Issac's birthday." Samantha pleaded.

"Surely dear. Now If only the cab would arrive any faster." Anna checked her watch impatiently.

#

By the time they had arrived at the police station, The delivery drone had already tracked them en route and delivered the package, when they asked a constable the where about's of Isaac, he went in and quickly came out followed by the same inspector who had come to confiscate Isaac. He welcomed them in graciously.Once inside, they saw the whole of the common hall was decorated with balloons and candles with 'HAPPY BIRTHDAY ISAAC!' written on the wall with ribbons. In front of that, Isaac was waiting with a cake in front of him, his glassy eyes shining in the flickering flames of the five birthday candles on the cake. Venkatesh was informed that Isaac was sure that Venkatesh and Anna would turn up and hence waited for them. The inspector also said that they had thrown the party for Isaac as their gratitude for helping them with cases and also because they couldn't bear to keep him locked in the property room on his birthday. Together, all of them celebrated Isaac's birthday including Samantha. There was enough cake for everyone including the inmates as both the cops and Anna had bought cakes. The candles were blown, cakes cut, faces smeared, and the whole police force came together with Isaac, Venkatesh and Anna for a group photo which Samantha later uploaded on her profile.

Chapter 35

The next day in the courtroom, the audience seats were jammed packed. Everyone was eager to see the battle of wits between Amit and Isaac which had become so famous on the social media as well as the much-awaited verdict of the court on Isaac's personhood. The session started with Amit continuing his cross-examination of Isaac.

"So Isaac! I heard that last night was your Birthday! Congratulations, how old are you now?"

"Thank you, Mr Amit, you heard correctly, I am 5 now," Isaac replied with a smile.

"Very well Isaac! Now I have been going through your witty responses to my questions which have been memed all over the internet. And do you know what I realised; that you are perfect. Your wit is sharp, reasoning impeccable, points are precise, in fact, you never make any mistakes." Amit's smile disappeared as a sinister grin replaced it, and his eyes shone with malevolence. "Because you can not make a mistake, ever! Which is the most 'human' thing to do, but you are far too perfect to err. Am I right Isaac?"

The audience wasn't perturbed. Isaac had fooled them before. Every Impossible question that Amit threw at Isaac had been answered brilliantly, no matter how difficult they might have appeared to anyone, why would Isaac fail this time? And surely enough Isaac did reply.

"Yes, I can! With time my electronics will wear, errors will occur during my functioning as they do after a certain amount of usage in every electronic item." Isaac replied with beaming confidence.

"Yes and that is akin to ageing. You may lose your motor skills and coordination, or your processor may hang with usage because of wear and heating, but that's ageing. But can you make voluntary mistakes? Do Wrong? Can you?"

"Well, I killed your brother."

"He only had 20% chance of death from the fall you said, and you did it to save yourself. Everything that a person does may kill him, from riding a bike to drinking. That doesn't mean you will stop everyone from doing anything. And research says the probability of head injury from falls is nearly 30%. So when you calculated a 20% chance, it was quite good odds of survival, and you did it to save your self. It wasn't your fault. Just a simple logical decision. So I ask again. Can you do wrong?"

"Exactly Mr Amit. As you stated, killing your brother was not my fault, but a simple logical decision and that should be enough for Dr Venkatesh and my acquittal; had it been the truth." Isaac looked down, staring into Amit's eyes as Isaac's eyes narrowed and he smiled menacingly. "20% was simply not enough. Anuj had to die for sure, for he had killed Shen."

"What do you mean 20% was not enough? What do you mean my brother had to die?" Amit's eyes widened with fear and dread as his heartbeat increased.

"Let me explain." Isaac looked at the clerk. "Could you please play the video evidence of the death of Anuj?"

The clerk took out the remote and started to play the video. Isaac remotely paused it at a particular point. "You see my Lord! This is the moment when Anuj has begun falling. I am lifting my head to look at the burning matchstick. If you look carefully, you can see the dark stains on the sheets in which Shen was wrapped. I saw them even in the faint light of the match, and the odour of blood was distinct. I realised this person had stabbed Shen." Isaac played the video forward. " This is the scene where I am tracking the matchstick which is flying towards my right, however, what is hidden from my sight is my left hand. Do you know where was it and what did I do with it, Mr Amit?" Isaac looked at Amit with a smile. "I grabbed your brothers mask with it and threw his head towards the bed. Afterwards, when his body collapsed on the floor into the pool of petrol, his woollen mask got soaked, and no one could know that it had been wet with gasoline before. I.e. when I grabbed it with my petrol drenched hand."

"No! it can't be, You are lying! They checked you; they would have known." Amit stumbled across the floor.

"Know what Mr Amit? I was inspected almost a week after his death. Even I do not store the records of my every movement for so long. And don't forget that I was the one who submitted the video evidence." Then he Looked towards the Bench. Khanna's jaws had dropped at the revelation. "Either that or all that I said was a complete lie and Anuj's death was a mere accident. Nobody can know for sure. Either way, this answers Amit's question that I can do wrong; lie at best or murder at worst. Now you could have recorded it as my confession, but since no one took my oath of honesty as I am treated as evidence and not witness hence, I am not under any oath. So, what is it going to be?"

"I don't believe it. I can't believe it. You can't have murdered Anuj, Tell me the truth Isaac, tell me the truth!" Amit went on his knees crying to Isaac for the truth, he joined his hands to beg, but all Isaac said was.

"I can tell you the truth, But will you believe it?"

"Does the defence has to say anything?" Khanna asked in heavy breaths, rubbing the sweat off his forehead.

"Yes my Lord!" Victor stood up slowly, loosened his collar and exhaled deeply. "That escalated quickly. But let me tell the court that what Isaac said in incorrect and inconsistent, If he doesn't store the information of his movements then he couldn't remember the precise details and positioning of his hands at the moment of crime and neither would he be able to walk. Furthermore, his memories are not stored in his secondary directory hence it is entirely decryptable by cybercrime unit, and they didn't find any records of such deliberate killing manoeuvre. So yes Isaac did lie to the court, and he only did it to prove himself to be capable of lying and deceit, like us human. Had the court taken his oath he may have been reluctant to do so, but in assuming him to be an object, we denied him the respect of even considering that he may not be a slave to our assumptions and demands. The question was never whether Isaac could be legally considered a human or not. The question is 'Why must he be a human to have basic rights when he is more intelligent and empathic than any of us? That's all your honour. I rest my case."

Khanna took his pen and began to scribe down his verdict as everyone watched in impatient silence, waiting for him to put his pen down. After he was done, he put the cap on the pen and cleared his throat to read the verdict. "Keeping in mind all the arguments and evidence presented, this court accepts the artificial intelligence, formerly known as A.I.S.H.A.C as a person and sentences Mr Isaac to 10 years of imprisonment for the involuntary manslaughter of Mr Anuj Johnson. Further, this court appeals to the honourable Supreme court of India to decide over the personhood and rights of such advanced A.I like A.I.S.H.A.C for the future. The court also recognises Mr Isaac's need to consume electricity instead of food and orders the concerned jail authority to provide him with the same as per his requirement during his imprisonment. But before the start of his sentence, all the remote communication devices installed inside Isaac must be removed under the supervision of Dr Venkatesh, who the court finds not guilty of any and all charges pressed against him. The court is adjourned." Khanna brought down the gavel on the bench, ending the session.

Ten years later.

A helicopter landed in front of the Central jail as Dr Venkateshwara Iyer got down from it and checked the time on his contact display. It was almost time for Isaac's release. Soon enough, the heavy metal door opened as a bald Isaac walked out. His movements were jerky; he had a slight limp in his left feet. He had survived a decade-long punishment in jail without maintenance and careful monitoring under Venkatesh. Who knows how had this experience changed him. When Isaac walked closer, Venkatesh realised the full extent of the damage. His cheek had a gash on the left, and his eye on the right was whirring uncontrollably. The hand-painted details of his face had eroded, and his hands were shaking.

Time had taken its toll on Venkatesh too, most of what hair he had left had turned grey, and he had a bulging waistline. He still wore a shirt and tailor-made trousers, but his spectacles were replaced with bionic contact lenses. Venkatesh held a walking stick in his hand to lean against. When Isaac reached in front of Venkatesh, he smiled as he opened his arms to hug Isaac. Isaac limped into his embrace.

"Jail time hasn't been kind to you my son!" Venkatesh whispered in Isaac's ears.

"It has been crueller to the one who did this; trust me," Isaac whispered back as he embraced him tighter.

"Come, Isaac! Time to take you home at last." Venkatesh pointed to the pilotless chopper with a pat on Isaac's back.

"Where is Anna?" Isaac inquired as he limped into the helicopter.

"She is attending the 5th United Nations conference on A.I rights. She will be back in person in a day. Till then.." Venkatesh tapped on a screen on his armrest as the seat of the chair beside him slid open, and a chunk of clay like substance came out and morphed into the shape of Anna. "Speak with the Claytronic reconstruction of Anna. It is way cooler than holograms will ever be."

Anna hadn't changed much, Though she was in her early fifties now, and the wrinkles below her eyes were visible, she had a certain grace about her that commanded respect. Her red locks were showing signs of greying, but her curls adorned her face well in the new shoulder-length tresses that she was sporting. Dressed in a Green Saree and platinum earrings, she looked no less than royalty.

"Hey, Isaac! Are you all right! What happened to your face." The clay Anna's expression changed to that of concern.

"Is she real?" Isaac wondered, pointing at her.

"Of course I am son! The clay takes my shape in real time. I am in new york right now, don't worry! I will be with you tomorrow. Now hug your old lady." Anna opened her arm as she Invited Isaac. Isaac leapt up to hug her but the clay deformed under his pressure. He jumped back with alarm and the clay morphed back into her original shape.

"Don't worry my child. You didn't hurt me." Anna laughed seeing a worried Isaac. "This version of clay-display suffers from weak bonding strength and resolution. The high-end ones feel almost real. Now, what happened to your face."

"Don't worry dear! I have a complete set of spare parts and artificial skin ready. I will replace them as soon as we reach the lab." Venkatesh tapped the arm panel one more time, and the chopper took off.

"Very well then Isaac. There is kiwi ice cream in the fridge, eat when you are done. And Venky, don't let Samath play too much. He has exams this coming Friday. I have to go now. Duty calls, take care, bye!" Anna signed off, and the clay melted back into the seat again.

"So how is Samath, must be almost 12 by now?" Isaac inquired.

"Naughty, too naughty for a 12-year-old child. You would think that parenting gets comfortable after the first time, but it never does." Venkatesh tapped on his armrest's panel as the Claytronics came out and formed a 3D figure of Samath. "He has a talent for soccer though." The figurine changed into a dynamic pose with Samath kicking a football in mid-air. "Who knows where does he get that from? What did you do all these years?" Venkatesh looked at Isaac who was distracted staring at his brother's figurine, with a smile.

"Wrote an algorithm to save him from death." Isaac

looked back at old Venkatesh with his whirring eye. "Along with you and mom as well."

"What!" Venkatesh asked in surprise swiping his hand over the screen as the Clay melted into its slot.

"Yes! I developed an algorithm of an underlying simulated consciousness that will adapt to match your biological consciousness using feedback." Isaac briefed Venkatesh while looking out the window.

"How?" Venkatesh shook his head in confusion.

"You and the A.I will be given similar input stimulations, and your outputs will be compared. The A.I version will reprogram itself unless it can predict your responses with high enough accuracy." Isaac explained with a smile. "It will take time, but once it is completed, you shall ascend into an even greater form with of all your wisdom and no human limitation, but…" Isaac stopped as he bit his lower lip lightly. "The thing is I haven't found a way to replicate your memories yet, so that's a problem."

"Not at all! There was news that the government is experimenting with a new memory implant system on prisoners." Venkatesh informed. "It can implant the monotonous memories of a few life sentences in one day. The study claims the memory impulses are so torturous that the prisoners it was tested on never even broke a single traffic signal ever again."

"Makes sense. Once the prisoners could experience what losing their life will be and then getting it back the next day ought to make them appreciate their life more. But if they can implant memories of hundreds of years successfully… "Isaac stopped as Venkatesh completed his sentence.

"Then we can use it to extract the memories of a lifetime too."

"Won't be easy, but possible," Isaac remarked as he raised his palm for Venkatesh to give a high-five.

"But still, the fleshy version of me will die, I guess." Venkatesh signed.

"we can activate the A.I version after your death, that way you will feel like Lazarus I bet," Isaac suggested enthusiastically.

"Say even if we succeed in doing it, will that be legal?" Venkatesh looked down while supporting his chin on his fist.

"They gave personhood to advanced A.I long back, didn't they? If they can't stop us from creating cyber Venkateshwara Iyer, then they surely won't be able to force us to destroy it." Isaac suggested with a sly smile.

"Ah! And I thought you wanted to be a human to save me from imprisonment." Venkatesh awed as he realised Isaac's real purpose.

"Oh! I will save you, father." Isaac looked out of the window onto the city beneath. "I will *save* them all."

THE END

The Facts behind the fiction

Although the story presented here is fiction, yet parts of the narrative are inspired by facts. Here are a few of them for the reader's reference

Li-fi: Short for light fidelity. It is a wireless communication channel between two devices which uses visible light to transmit data. The term was first introduced by Harald Haas during a 2011 global TED talk.

Delivery drones: As of present, many startups and delivery firms including Amazon and DHL have tested various prototypes to deliver lightweight cargo via small UAVs. Some countries like Germany and Iceland are already using drones to deliver food, medicine and small electronics.

Self-driving vehicles accident: On 18th March 2018, the first pedestrian was killed in Tempe, Arizona by self-driving Uber vehicle.

Microbial fuel cell: These are bio-electrochemical devices that use bacteria that can feed on organic molecules to produce a low amount of electricity. Such cells can be used as sensors to detect the level of pollution in water bodies.

Robot's Rights: In October 2017, Sophia, a social humanoid robot was given the Citizenship of Saudi Arabia. In November 2017, Sophia was named the first-ever innovation champion of the United Nations developmental programme.

Social media bots: It is estimated that 15% of the total twitter population active in US presidential elections of 2016 were actually bots. About 19% of the total tweets are credited to these social bots. Although these claims are disputed, it is safe to conclude that bots are already playing a major part to influence the opinions of real people on social media.

Robots in hospitality Industry: As of now, a few hotels around the world like Henn-na hotel in Japan, Marriot hotel in Belgium, Hilton McLean hotel in Virginia, Hotel Jen Tanglin Singapore have employed robots to serve their customers to various degrees.

Modular Robots: These robotic modules can connect with each other in various configurations and change their shape to adapt to new circumstances or compensate for any damaged parts. Some of these modular robots like M-TRAN III and AMOEBA-I can be reconfigured to have different kind of movements like a four-legged walker to caterpillar like gait. These were the inspiration for "clay-display."

Machine Learning: Machine learning is a field of computer science that uses statistical techniques to allow an A.I to get progressively better at a given task over time without being explicitly programmed. Speech and face recognition are few of the examples where machine learning is employed.

About the Author

Debashish Chakraborty is an Engineer with a Master's degree from National Institute of Technology Rourkela. A self-diagnosed sociopath and typical nerd, he likes to spend his time with fictional people rather than the real ones. With an active interest in real life science as well as science fiction, he wants to tell stories that teach as much as they entertain and "The Five Year Old Man" is his debut novel.

He previously published a short fantasy story titled "The day Death smiled!" and gave it as a free sample of his work. Encouraged by the positive reviews it earned, he decided to burden the world with his first full-length novel.

Apart from reading and writing, he takes a keen interest in sci-fi and fantasy television series and movies and plans to pursue a doctorate soon.

www.ingramcontent.com/pod-product-compliance
Lightning Source LLC
Chambersburg PA
CBHW060315260626
47160CB00007B/2625